S0-BYO-598

"Shower later. You and me now..."

"You smell delicious," Troy whispered as he kissed Darcy's bare shoulder, the base of her neck, her throat. "I want you now. No waiting..."

His hunger grew as he undid his jeans, pushing until they fell to his ankles and then stepping out of them. Finally, he found her mouth, wrapped her tightly in his arms and lifted her, making her clutch at his shoulders and moan against his lips.

Yes.

She wanted him, this stunning, incredibly hot, mysterious woman. She wasn't as indifferent as her methodical striptease had suggested.

His ego swelled along with other parts.

He was going to make this good for her, good enough to break through that iron control.

So what if she hadn't told him anything about herself? She'd tell him plenty with her body by the time this night was over....

Dear Reader,

Have you ever locked eyes with a stranger and felt deep emotion you can't explain away as simple attraction? Given that love develops over time, that it involves two people knowing and accepting each other completely, the concept of love at first sight seems dubious. But how else to explain that intense reaction?

For beautiful restaurateur Darcy Clark and sexy tech-guy/triathlete Troy Cahill, the third and final hero and heroine of my Checking E-Males miniseries, this thunderbolt of desire leaves them with no clue how to fit all the new and tempestuous emotions into what they think they know about love and relationships. It was great fun to watch them squirm and try to avoid the obvious truth. Also in this book, our beloved master matchmaker, Marie, owner of Milwaukeedates.com, gets another stab at convincing the charming Quinn Peters that she doesn't remind him of his sister after all…

I hope you've enjoyed the first two books in this series, *Turn Up the Heat* and *Long Slow Burn,* and that you'll consider *Hot to the Touch* an appropriate send-off for Candy, Kim, Darcy and Marie. I'll really miss these women!

Cheers,

Isabel Sharpe

www.IsabelSharpe.com

Isabel Sharpe

HOT TO THE TOUCH

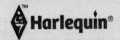

TORONTO NEW YORK LONDON
AMSTERDAM PARIS SYDNEY HAMBURG
STOCKHOLM ATHENS TOKYO MILAN MADRID
PRAGUE WARSAW BUDAPEST AUCKLAND

If you purchased this book without a cover you should be aware
that this book is stolen property. It was reported as "unsold and
destroyed" to the publisher, and neither the author nor the
publisher has received any payment for this "stripped book."

Recycling programs
for this product may
not exist in your area.

ISBN-13: 978-0-373-79623-6

HOT TO THE TOUCH

Copyright © 2011 by Muna Shehadi Sill

All rights reserved. Except for use in any review, the reproduction or
utilization of this work in whole or in part in any form by any electronic,
mechanical or other means, now known or hereafter invented, including
xerography, photocopying and recording, or in any information storage
or retrieval system, is forbidden without the written permission of the
publisher, Harlequin Enterprises Limited, 225 Duncan Mill Road,
Don Mills, Ontario, Canada M3B 3K9.

This is a work of fiction. Names, characters, places and incidents are
either the product of the author's imagination or are used fictitiously,
and any resemblance to actual persons, living or dead, business
establishments, events or locales is entirely coincidental.

This edition published by arrangement with Harlequin Books S.A.

For questions and comments about the quality of this book
please contact us at Customer_eCare@Harlequin.ca.

® and TM are trademarks of the publisher. Trademarks indicated with
® are registered in the United States Patent and Trademark Office, the
Canadian Trade Marks Office and in other countries.

www.Harlequin.com

Printed in U.S.A.

ABOUT THE AUTHOR

Isabel Sharpe was not born pen in hand like so many of her fellow writers. After she quit work to stay home with her firstborn son and nearly went out of her mind, she started writing. After more than twenty novels for Harlequin—along with another son—Isabel is more than happy with her choice these days. She loves hearing from readers. Write to her at www.IsabelSharpe.com.

Books by Isabel Sharpe

HARLEQUIN BLAZE
  11—THE WILD SIDE
  76—A TASTE OF FANTASY*
126—TAKE ME TWICE*
162—BEFORE I MELT AWAY
186—THRILL ME**
221—ALL I WANT...†
244—WHAT HAVE I DONE FOR ME LATELY?
292—SECRET SANTA
         "The Nights Before Christmas"
376—MY WILDEST RIDE††
393—INDULGE ME‡
444—NO HOLDING BACK
533—WHILE SHE WAS SLEEPING...‡‡
539—SURPRISE ME...‡‡
595—TURN UP THE HEAT§
606—LONG SLOW BURN§
619—HOT TO THE TOUCH§

*Men to Do
**Do Not Disturb
†The Wrong Bed
††The Martini Dares
‡Forbidden Fantasies
‡‡The Wrong Bed: Again & Again
§Checking E-Males

To Sienna, Ruby and Leia,
who have made life so much cheerier.

Prologue

"CAN WE TALK ABOUT SOMETHING other than men?" Darcy flipped back her dark hair, an impatient scowl marring her beautiful features. "I think I'm getting heartburn."

Across the table, Marie Hewitt watched her carefully. Every month the four of them, restaurant owner and chef Darcy Clark, plus web designer Kim Horton, event planner Candy Graham and herself, CEO of Milwaukeedates.com, gathered for this third-Wednesday breakfast meeting of Women in Power, Milwaukee's organization of female business owners. Since Marie started her matchmaking campaign in January for her three younger, never-married friends, Candy and Kim had fallen. Candy and Justin Case had become engaged back in February on a wonderful if slightly out of control Valentine's day. Nathan Alexander had asked Kim to marry him the previous month, on April fifteenth, her thirtieth birthday.

Until now, Darcy had seemed genuinely thrilled for them, though stubbornly resistant to any and all attempts to entice her into signing up for Marie's online dating company in order to find her own happiness. Could her sudden irritability have anything to do with envy? Was she finally cracking, and would a little of her suppressed longing for love start oozing out? Marie was counting on that happening eventually. Darcy's

I-hate-men act might fool some people, but the more she saw, the less Marie was buying it.

"Sorry." Kim put her hand on Darcy's arm, eyes warm with contrition. "I know Candy and I are being nauseating going on about wedding plans when we're all here to talk business. Tell us how life was last month in the restaurant world. Though I keep hearing people raving about Gladiolas so I probably don't need to ask how it's doing."

"Things are okay." Darcy settled her coffee mug back on the table. "Do you all remember Raoul?"

Kim made a disgusted face. "The slimeball you fired? The one who was having the affair with the married waitress, stole from the restaurant and came on to you to try and get professional favors?"

Darcy nodded grimly. "Yup. That slimeball."

"What about him?" Marie went on alert. "He's not still trying to land you, is he?"

"Worse. He's starting his own restaurant. Emphasis on local and organic while keeping prices affordable. A short, seasonal menu and daily specials with whimsical names. Sound familiar?"

"Sounds exactly like Gladiolas." Candy looked helplessly furious. "What a scum. That is disgusting."

"Ya think?" Darcy shrugged. "Who knows, word has it his investor might back out. I hope so."

"We all hope so," Candy said. "But if he doesn't, after the restaurant opens we'll plant roaches and rats in the kitchen, then report Raoul to the health inspector."

"Oh, good one." Kim patted Candy's shoulder affectionately. "How about I post viciously negative reviews all over the internet?"

"Very nice, Kim." Marie smiled her approval. "I'll book the whole place every night and then cancel at the last minute."

"Thanks, guys." Darcy grinned warmly. It was great to see

her smile. She didn't do so often enough. "Look, I didn't mean to rain on the wedding parade before. I don't know where that came from. PMS probably."

Marie smirked. PMS? Nuh-uh. Though Darcy would probably be the last to figure it out.

"No, no, you were absolutely right." Candy gracefully waved away the apology; Justin's ring, which he'd planted in a delivery pizza, flashed on her left hand. "We were being disgusting. You and Marie must be ready to scream."

"Not me." Marie pulled off the crisp end of her croissant and spread jam on it. "I'm delighted. And I know Darcy is, too."

"Yes. I really am." Darcy nodded emphatically. "If you guys are happy that's—"

"However, she is also ragingly jealous." Marie bit casually into her pastry, counting down to Darcy's anticipated explosion. Three…two…one…

"Jealous!" Darcy cracked up too loudly. "Oh, right. Deep down I really want my own self-centered man-child keeping me enslaved for the rest of my life."

She laughed again harshly, grabbed her mug and gripped it between her palms as if it was her salvation.

"Jeez, Darcy." Candy frowned at her. "Could you turn up the bitterness a little more? I'm not sure it's coming across."

"Nathan and Justin aren't like that." Kim's soft tone was uncharacteristically firm.

"They're all like that." Darcy's voice broke. She jerked the mug to her lips and took a sip.

"Not all of them." Marie spoke gently, heart aching for her friend. Would Darcy ever admit she needed someone in her life to help share her burdens, to help her open up and trust again? Would she ever admit that in the midst of a full and successful life she was isolated and lonely? "With the right man, you'll never feel that you're—"

"No." Darcy held up her hand. "I'm not going there, Marie. Find someone else if you need to keep foisting women onto lonely men. I like my freedom, making my own decisions. I take care of myself and of Gladiolas. I don't have time or energy for another guy to make the whole relationship about him and his needs, and to hell with mine."

"I understand." Marie waited a beat, then met Kim's blue eyes, which were helpless with worry, and Candy's brown ones, dark with frustration. She smiled reassuringly. They'd get Darcy to fall somehow, sooner or later.

Maybe not overtly, by making her an appointment at Milwaukeedates.com, the way Marie had been able to with Candy and Kim. Maybe not by making reasonable overtures and putting forth reasonable logic. Some other method.

The Women in Power president came to the podium and called the room to order. Members finished sentences and cups of coffee, turned their chairs and settled in to pay attention.

Marie folded her arms on the table, her gaze focused on the back of Darcy's dark head. There would be some chink, some fault line, some way into the warmth and passion Darcy kept bottled up out of fear, and Marie was going to find it, no matter how much resistance Darcy mustered.

She lowered her brows thoughtfully, imagining the profile she'd love to put up for Darcy on Milwaukeedates.com. Men would fall all over themselves wanting her. Eventually the right one would come along, a man strong and secure enough to let Darcy be the woman she needed to be, if only Darcy would give him a chance.

The president introduced the morning's speaker and with the applause the glimmer of an idea rose into Marie's mind and floated enticingly, even as she knew she'd have to reject it for ethical reasons.

Though when it came to Darcy, maybe ethics were beside the point. Maybe the only way Marie could win this battle against stubborn denial was to get stubborn herself. Stubborn and persistent.

Stubborn, persistent and willing to fight dirty.

1

"RADISHES." DARCY TAPPED HER PENCIL on the gleaming wooden bar, made from salvaged Wisconsin oak. Her thoughts were drifting from Gladiolas's emptying dining room around her to the side dish she was imagining for her restaurant's summer menu, though it being merely the end of May in Wisconsin, summer seemed depressingly far away. Sauteed radishes, smoothed with butter, accented with salt and chives. And something else…sugar snap peas for color, texture and to balance the slight bite with sweetness. Or would a complementing strong taste be better, to deepen the flavor? Chard? Watercress?

"Radishes sound perfect for my mood."

Darcy snapped out of her vegetable reverie and squinted at Amy Walker, her dining room manager. "What mood, crunchy?"

"Round and bitter." Amy tipped back the last of the cup of coffee she never seemed to be without. Her plump body was slumped onto her stool, her short, flaming red ponytail shedding strands that hung around her cheeks.

"Bitter? I like that. Maybe we can use that in a menu name. 'Love failed me—I'm bitter.' A pork dish with bitter orange, a side of greens and radishes, something like that." She made a few notes on a paper in front of her, then remembered they were talking about Amy. "Sorry, my brain went AWOL. Why are you bitter? Not Colin…"

"He hasn't called for two days or answered my emails. I'm thinking I've worked my Amy-magic again and am being dumped."

"No way." Darcy felt familiar anger churn in her stomach. Yes, she had issues, but it was hard to work through them when men kept providing more and more examples of selfish behavior. "I thought this guy was really into you."

"Yeah, me, too." Amy laughed harshly. "And they say *women* play mind games and are hard to figure out."

"I'm sorry. But you know men. They have a completely bizarre concept of time. He'll reappear when you least expect it, without a clue he'd left you hanging." Darcy pushed her untouched glass of chardonnay over to her friend, and signaled their handsome, burly bartender, Jeff, to get her another. "In the meantime, drink away your sorrows, honey. At least alcohol is dependable."

"And a depressant." Amy lifted the glass anyway and took a healthy swallow. "I don't know. It's too easy to blame men. Sometimes I think it's just me, Ms. Man-Poison."

"You are *not*—"

"No, really, I'm serious. I think there's something about me that horrifies them. Until I find out what that is, maybe there's no point looking anymore. I'm thinking of giving up."

"No." Darcy held up a hand for emphasis. "*I'm* the cynical, damaged one. *I'm* the one headed for a life of questionable hygiene, living alone in a ramshackle house overrun with cats. Not you."

"Maybe." Amy fingered the stem of her wineglass, eyes down. "I want to find a guy who accepts me, warts and all, who'll consciously work on the relationship and compromise when necessary, someone for whom my happiness is nearly as important as his. Because that's exactly what I'd do for him."

"Oh, *that* guy!" Darcy accepted her new wine from Jeff. "I know exactly where he is."

"Where?" Amy lifted a skeptical brow.

"Hanging out with Santa Claus and the Easter Bunny!"

Amy snorted. "I know, I know. But I can't totally crush hope the way you have. I wish I could. It would save me a lot of trouble and a lot of pain. I really thought Colin would hang around. Of course I probably thought that about all of them at one time."

"Uh…yeah." Darcy nudged her affectionately. "Didn't we all."

"It's just that it *can* happen, out of the blue, when you least expect it. My sister met her husband on her millionth blind date, sick to death of trying to find someone, and they were both struck stupid with love the second they saw each other. They're still wildly happy."

"Because they're stupid. You said it yourself."

Amy finally loosened up enough to let out her trademark cascade of giggles. "I did. Now enough of my whining. Back to your radishes."

"Nah." Darcy lifted her glass, irritated by the story of Amy's sister. People who were disgustingly goopy like that made her sick. Or jealous. Sometimes she wasn't sure which. "Forget the radishes for now. We need to cheer you up first."

"Good luck."

"Ooh, I know. Ken, the new Lenson's sales rep, came by this morning with industry gossip." Darcy sipped her wine. She'd stick to the gossip that had been pleasant. The rest had been eating at her all day. "The new place down National near Fourth Street? Esmee? The chef is Lebanese. He's supposedly giving the usual bar food an innovative Middle Eastern kick. Want to check it out? Get your mind off Colin?"

"Oh, that would be—" Amy's cell rang with the theme to *Love Story*. She fished it out of her pocket and gasped at the display. "It's *him*."

"Ha!" Darcy smacked the bar with her palm, wanting to tell Amy not to answer it. "Told you he'd show up."

"Oh, my gosh." Amy took a deep breath, smoothing her hair, and connected the call. "Hey, Colin! How are you? Good. Yes, I'm fine. But I was worried, since I haven't heard—"

Darcy shook her head urgently. Rule number one: never let a guy think you've been sitting around waiting for his call.

Amy cringed and nodded understanding. "Heard from my family in a while and was thinking you were one of them checking in."

Darcy gave her a thumbs-up.

"Uh-huh. As far as I know. Oh, tonight?" She looked pleadingly at Darcy. "I'm, um…"

Darcy shook her head again, hard enough that her bobbed hair flew out nearly horizontal. Rule number two: Never be immediately available to a guy who hasn't been available to you.

"I'd love to." Amy spoke firmly, turning away from Darcy who rolled her eyes. "I've *really* missed you."

Darcy let out a sound of disgust purposely loud enough for Amy to hear.

"Yes. I know where that is. Okay. Yes. See you in a few." She shut her phone with a soft sigh.

"*Amy*. At least pretend you haven't been panting after his call for—"

"I know." She held up a hand to stop Darcy's lecture. "I know."

"Seriously, if you want men to stop taking you for granted…" She tried to soften the frustration in her voice. "You have to show them you're worth better treatment."

"Yes. But as I said, I have *really* missed him." She slid

off the stool and squeezed Darcy's shoulder. "You're right. I know you are. In a week or a month I'll be miserable over him again. I just—"

"Have *really* missed him."

"Wow, how did you know?" Amy looked like a different person, cheeks flushed, eyes snapping excitement. Even her hair had revived.

"Wild guess." Darcy managed a smile. "Go. Have fun. He doesn't deserve you."

"Undoubtedly. And I'll be screwed over in the end. It's what men do to me. Then you can say, 'Ha-ha, told you so,' and watch in amazement at my masochistic stupidity while I proceed to do it all again with someone else."

"Gee, um, I'm really looking forward to that." Darcy rolled her eyes in exaggerated dismay. "Wouldn't it be easier to stay single?"

"Easier, yes. Better? No." Amy jumped off the bar stool and strode over to their hostess, Kelly, to ask her to close up.

Darcy watched her go. Easier, but not better... She turned resolutely away and pushed her glass to the bartender. "G'night, Jeff."

"'Night, chef. You heading out?"

"Yeah. New place to try tonight." Darcy had to force the enthusiasm, when she generally loved discovering neighborhood gems. She didn't mind going out alone, either. In fact, sometimes she preferred the opportunity to concentrate on the food instead of on making conversation.

But tonight...

Among the gossip Ken passed along was that Raoul, Darcy's unlamented ex-employee, had secured new wads of cash for his restaurant after the original investor had indeed backed out. James Thomas, one of Milwaukee's wealthiest, had turned Darcy down for Gladiolas, saying women had no place in the restaurant business. She'd had to settle for a lesser amount from the bank, which meant shelving plans for a more elegant downtown address and locating Gladiolas where she could afford to lease.

"Sounds good. Report back." Jeff, classic stud of few words, acknowledged a patron's signal and went over to refill his drink.

Darcy slid off her stool and strode through the dining room and into the gleaming stainless kitchen she was so proud of, inhaling the fragrance of food in its many stages of preparation. She collected her things and called out a good-night to the staff, including Gladiolas's dishwasher, real name Francis McDonald, but everyone called him Ace. Great kid, reliable, could be pulled onto the line when things got crazy busy in the kitchen, but from what Darcy could tell, he lived most of the time in a chemically enhanced universe.

She banged out the alley door, got into her car and drove down National Avenue from her own place on Fourteenth Street to Fourth. Short hop, but she'd been on her feet all day, and while she wouldn't mind walking over, after a drink and some food, she'd want to get home quickly to her tiny house in Washington Heights, which she'd bought five years earlier after saving every cent she could for the downpayment.

Too bad Amy hadn't wanted to come tonight. Another wonderful, funny, smart, talented friend wasted on the male population of Milwaukee. Maybe Darcy should introduce Amy to Milwaukeedates.com owner, Marie Hewitt, who'd matched up two of the town's best and brightest, Candy and Kim. But talking to Marie about matching up Amy would invariably segue into Marie talking about matching up Darcy, and sorry, but Darcy couldn't be less interested. Though seeing Amy so happy when Colin called…

Nuh-uh, she wasn't going there. Some women could find happiness in men. Darcy wasn't one of them. The guys she fell for were angry, controlling and uninterested in supporting her, especially her ambition. Someone had to break that pattern and protect her, and Darcy had nominated herself for the job. Once in a while she allowed herself the luxury of a one-night stand or a casual series of dates, but she drew the line there. Any longer and it became apparent men wanted women who were home for them every night, not out on the front lines battling for their own success. Recently Darcy had also been denying herself those brief encounters. Even those had become dangerous to her sanity.

She found the restaurant and parked on a side street, emerged into the too-chilly air and hurried into the small, warm, welcoming space whose dim lighting created nice intimacy. A clean but battered wooden bar, kept on from the Irish pub this place used to be, dominated the room, furnished with booths and a few tables. Nearly every table and booth was taken, the bar three-quarters full. A good sign, though Darcy was attracting more attention than she liked from the mostly male clientele, even wearing an outfit about as revealing as a Girl Scout's, an outfit which also happened to be pretty ripe from an evening sweating in the kitchen.

Three stools sat empty at the end of the bar. Darcy chose the nearest to the door, leaving two unoccupied seats next to her, hoping no one would sit in search of a chatting partner.

"Hi, there." Nice-looking bartender, big guy, middle-aged, with warm gray eyes. Ten years and thirty pounds ago, he would have been a serious temptation. "What can I get you?"

"Arak, please."

He broke into a smile, bushy eyebrows raised, and responded in Arabic.

"No, no." Darcy shook her head regretfully. "Not native. I just know the drink."

"Ah, okay. Coming right up."

"What didja order? Ah-rack?" The pink-faced guy to her right looked as if he'd been at the bar most of the week.

"Arak. Anise liquor. Very dry. Very good."

He made a face. "Anise, like licorice? Licorice is candy. Sissy drink."

Darcy snorted. Said he who was drinking rum and Coke.

"Enjoy." The bartender set in front of her a glass of clear liquid, another of ice and a small carafe of water. "Like a menu?"

"Definitely." She ignored Mr. Sissy Drink, who was still muttering about alcoholic candy. Darcy would love to see him try to walk straight after a couple of glasses of arak. Strong as well as delicious.

"Here you go." The bartender handed her a menu.

Darcy opened it and fell in love. Burgers, salads, sandwiches and pizzas, but in each category a twist. You could have a burger with ketchup, mustard and pickle, or with parsley, onion, cinnamon and tahini sauce. Pizza with cheese and sausage or with ground lamb, diced red peppers and halloumi cheese. Iceberg salad with shredded cheddar, croutons and ranch dressing or romaine with toasted pita and feta, dressed with olive oil, garlic and mint.

After a terrible time deciding, she succumbed to the lamb pizza and the romaine salad. The bartender brought her a small bowl of olives, a few tiny round loaves of pita, about the diameter of tangerines, and a dish of a soft creamy white cheese with the tang of yogurt.

Darcy poured water into her arak, which turned it pearly-white, and added a few cubes of ice. She took a small gulp and sighed in pleasure. The anise flavor was clear and light, beautifully refreshing. A few sips later, she mingled the taste with a mouthful of bread stuffed with cheese and an olive. Heaven.

As usual, the experience of good food relaxed her, and she

felt ready to check out her surroundings. Good crowd for a Wednesday night. A few couples on dates, a few single men at the bar, groups of guys out for a guy-time, one table of women. Most were neat and presentable, not too different from the crowd she attracted to Gladiolas. Neighborhood people out for the night. What crowd would Raoul get with his fancy backer and address? High prices would mean clientele with money to burn and similarly situated friends who had friends, who had friends…

Movement caught her eye, and she realized she'd been staring at a good-looking guy in a red shirt drinking with friends; he leered and toasted her with his beer.

Ugh. The last thing she needed was some guy thinking she was out trolling for the same thing he was.

Her food came, a happy distraction. The aroma made her stomach growl and her hand reach eagerly for a slice of the pizza, which she immediately launched toward her mouth.

Mmm. The crust was charred appetizingly around the edges, the lamb and peppers fragrant and subtly spiced, the cheese tender, mild and sparingly used so its bland richness didn't overwhelm the dish.

Delicious. After a few more ravenous bites, she gathered a forkful of the fresh-looking salad, preparing to dive in.

"So I was wondering…" A man's shape entered her peripheral vision. Red shirt. Ugh again. He leaned on the bar next to her, too close, talking too loudly. His too-sweet aftershave intruded on her smell and taste. "Has anyone ever mentioned that you look like Catherine Zeta-Jones?"

"Yes." She glanced at him witheringly. "And they didn't get anywhere, either."

"Hey, now, don't be like that." His ingratiating grin didn't falter, if anything he was talking louder. She became aware that they were attracting interest from Pink-Faced Sissy-Drink two stools to her right, and from the guy's table of friends; she wanted to drop to all fours and growl threateningly. "Give me a break here. I'm a nice guy."

"I'm sure you are, but I'm only interested in food tonight."

"Aw, c'mon. Help me out here, beautiful. I bet my friends that I could buy you a drink."

"Really?" She picked up her arak, sipped it leisurely. "Sorry, you lost that one."

"I'm Jay." He winked. "And I never lose."

"First time for everything."

He chuckled and leaned in. "Seriously, I'm harmless. Just want to buy you a drink. You won't regret—"

"I already do." She turned deliberately toward him. "Go away."

"Wow." He stared at her for a few seconds, then gave a bitter chuckle. "You're a bitch, you know that?"

"Yup." Darcy held his gaze calmly. "But it's better than being a buttwipe."

He left, but not before he called Darcy another of her least favorite words. What a jerk.

She turned back to her dinner, having to force herself to resume eating, which was the jerk's worst offense, because the food was damn good. Halfway through the pizza and salad, two-thirds of the way through her arak and undisturbed further, she managed to regain her composure.

"I'm *outta* here." The pink-faced guy seemed to be talking to no one in particular. He moved off his stool and for a second, Darcy expected him to hit the floor, slumped like a sack of potatoes. Miraculously he managed to stay upright.

The bartender reached to shake his hand. "See ya, Fred."

"See ya tomorrow." Fred wobbled behind Darcy toward the door. She hoped he wasn't driving.

"Another arak?"

Darcy looked up to decline, but while the bartender was

standing in front of her, he was asking the guy who'd been sitting three chairs down, just to the right of Pink-Faced Guy. Darcy turned to see who else was drinking the ambrosia of Lebanon.

He was dark, but his features looked too Waspy to be Arabic. Handsome, several years younger than she was, she'd guess mid-twenties, dressed in a dark shirt and black jeans that showed his body to be tall, lean and nicely shaped. Well, well. Male candy. Too bad she'd put herself on a diet.

The bartender put a new glass of arak in front of him. He lifted the carafe of water to pour with very nice hands, strong-looking, fingers long and masculine, nails blunt and clean. Definitely an attractive—

He turned and met her eyes. Darcy froze with her arak halfway to her mouth. An electric storm sprang to life in her chest, spread to her stomach, down her torso, tingling through her arms and legs. Immediately, she glanced away. Then back, unable to resist. He was still watching her; his impossibly dark and deep eyes made it tough to breathe or think. *What the hell was that?*

She forced her attention back to her meal, but could only gaze at it, as if waiting for the food to rise up and eat her instead.

Instant lust, instant attraction. Sure Darcy had experienced those before, but never like this. She must be feeling particularly vulnerable tonight? Tired? On edge? Ovulating? She wanted to look again, felt almost compelled to, but there was fear she'd be giving something away, something very important she had to keep.

Like mental stability.

A deep breath, and she made herself eat salad, fragrant with mint, bold with garlic. The bite of vinegar and the soothing fruit of olive oil grounded her. This was real. This was what she'd come here for. Another bite of pizza, and she managed to finish the slice, finish the salad, finish her drink, feeling the man's pull throughout, fighting her desire to look again, to see if he was watching her. To see if he'd felt even half of what she had.

She pulled out her wallet, resisting the urge to order another drink, to linger and taunt herself with what could be possible. It was late. Another long day tomorrow.

"Leaving?"

Darcy's hand stilled in the act of pulling out her credit card. She turned, braced this time for the impact of those eyes. The preparation didn't help much. She felt as if her body had gone into overdrive. Shaky overdrive. Shaky, helpless overdrive. "Thought I would."

"Can I buy you another drink instead?"

She didn't move. If he bought her a drink, they'd start talking. She'd get a pretty serious buzz from more arak, dangerous around this powerful chemistry. She'd want to spend the night with him. Inevitably, the sex would be hot, satisfying and for one night her problems could be pushed aside, along with her responsibilities. For one night she'd be part of something bigger than just herself.

But then she might wake up with that horrible empty longing again, the grief she never admitted to anyone she'd had, the one she didn't even like to acknowledge to herself. Last time the morning after had been so hard, she'd promised herself no more one-night stands. Sex was lovely, but she wouldn't die without it. Though now that she'd met this man, she might.

"No?"

Darcy blinked, aware she was taking an absurdly long time to respond.

"Or…yes?" His very sexy lips curved in a small smile. *Oh, that mouth.*

One drink. One drink wouldn't hurt. Nor would another night she didn't have to spend alone. She put her wallet away,

got down from the stool and sauntered toward him, hand held
out in anticipation of touching his. Of touching him.

"Yes."

2

"HOW ABOUT THAT ONE, OVER there? The tall one?" Justin nudged Troy and pointed to a trio of women who'd just walked into Esmee Restaurant, where he and Justin were sitting at the bar. "She's hot. More than that, she looks nice."

Troy turned and gave a cursory look. The female in question was taller than her companions, probably five-eight or nine, blonde and attractive, dressed provocatively. He nodded wearily. Yes, Justin, she was hot. Yes, Justin, she looked nice. No, Justin, Troy wasn't going to offer to take her out, because for all Troy knew, she was newly released from the cozy facilities at Milwaukee County Mental Health. Plus, Troy already had his eye on a woman at the Milwaukee Athletic Club, though he hadn't mentioned that to Justin in case he and Candy arranged a double wedding before Troy even got up the nerve to ask Missy for a first date.

Justin was a good friend, had been since they were in college together at UCLA—in fact, Justin had moved from California to Milwaukee after Troy invited the talented writer to be his coauthor on an interactive computer manual they'd finished last month. Troy couldn't blame Justin for his…enthusiasm when it came to matchmaking. For one thing, he was over-the-top in love with his fiancée, Candy, and was therefore in that blissful state where he wanted everyone else to be as happy for the same reason. For another, Justin had made the acquaintance of arak tonight, liquor Troy's half-Lebanese friend Chad had turned Troy on to. The stuff was delicious, but lethal, about fifty-percent alcohol. Not that Justin was in danger of embarrassing himself, but he was definitely feeling no pain. Good thing Candy had an event nearby and was showing up shortly to drive him home.

"Oh, wait, never mind." Justin waved away the concept of the blonde with obvious irritation. "She's too young."

"What defines too young?"

Justin leaned over confidentially. "Jonas Brothers T-shirt."

"Ooh, yeah." Troy hid his amusement. "Way too young."

"Don't worry, man." Justin sipped arak and thumped his glass down on the bar. "We'll find you someone. Sooner or later."

"We?"

"We." Justin pointed to himself. "We'll find you someone who will light you up the second you lay eyes on her. Who makes every nerve ending in your body come to life in a way you've never felt before, ever, not even close. It's like life-heat, it's like...the hotness of life. It's like you're—"

"Seriously sloshed. Listen to yourself, buddy."

"I know. But it's true. It happened to me." He thumped his chest proudly. "I looked into Candy's eyes and thought... whoa. This is it. This is her. I just met the rest of my life."

"That's what you were thinking? Really?"

Justin frowned. "Okay, maybe not consciously. Consciously I was thinking she had nice eyes and a nice mouth. And legs. Great legs. Even her feet are sexy. And her—"

"Okay, dude." Troy socked him in the shoulder. "That's plenty, thanks."

"I love good feet on a woman, too." The voice came from the guy on the stool to Troy's left; he looked as if he'd been in the sun all day, though more likely he'd been here in the bar all day. "Good feet and good lips. Good hands and sturdy hips."

"Poetry." Justin beamed at him across Troy. "Lips and hips. I love it."

"Thanks." The guy went abruptly back to staring at his drink as if someone had turned his power off.

Troy rubbed his hand over his face. When was Justin's fiancée coming?

"I may sound over-the-top when I talk about Candy, but I'm telling you, being in love is the greatest. Really in love, not the torture you went through with Drama Queen Debby and that I went through with Attention-Needing Angie—"

"Yeah. Yeah, I know." Troy was getting impatient with the topic. "And I appreciate your concern."

Justin shrugged. "I'm just one of many who wants to see you happy."

"Dude, I *am* happy." He raised his hand to cut off Justin's immediate protest. "Yes, someday I'll meet someone and have my nerve endings incinerate me with their life-heat or whatever you said, and I'll be more happy. But right now life is good. Our book is in, the publisher is ecstatic, we have some time before we have to start the next one. I'm finally over Debby, have done some dating. This is all good stuff. I'm not in any hurry to change it."

"Okay." Justin nodded solemnly and drained his glass. "I'll back off. But I warn you, Candy's been looking out for you, too. And when she gets an idea…"

Troy laughed. "Uh-huh."

"Speaking of." He held up his wrist, squinting to bring his watch face into focus. "She'll be here any second. I should wait outside so she doesn't have to park. You coming?"

"Nah." Troy didn't want to go home yet. Lately his house had been feeling empty, without the crush of working on the book on top of his regular day job. He'd been training for the next triathlon in September with Chad, going out with friends, playing basketball on Sundays, taking his golden chow mix, Dylan, for long walks, all of which helped, but they didn't fill the house. "I'll stay and finish my drink."

"Okay." Justin slapped him on the back and slid clumsily off the stool. "Just keep your eyes open."

The man with the red face turned his power switch back on. "And check out her feet."

Troy considered moving away, but after Justin disappeared, the guy receded again into staring at his glass of Coke, which Troy would guess was healthily dosed with rum. Booze and caffeine, upper and downer taken together. No wonder the guy looked as if he were in suspended animation.

The front door opened; Troy glanced over, half-expecting Justin or Candy, and did a double take, along with half the bar. The male half.

A woman. Older than he was, early thirties. Dark. Beautiful. Stop-traffic beautiful. Reduce-men-to-drooling-idiocy beautiful, even dressed in black shapeless pants and a black shapeless shirt, neither of which could hide that she was all shape underneath.

"Would ya look at *that*." The little man beside him voiced what every straight guy in the place must be thinking.

She seemed completely at ease, undoubtedly used to being stared at, headed for the bar and sat at the corner, leaving two seats between her and Troy's red-faced neighbor. In a rich, musical voice she ordered arak and Arabic food—was she Lebanese? Troy watched her surreptitiously—watched her pour her drink and sip it reverentially, watched her after her food came, lips and teeth taking bites, face registering pleasure—and found himself getting turned on. Maybe it had been too long, maybe Justin was right, and he should try to make a move on Little Miss Jonas Brothers. Not the woman he wanted, but this one was way out of his league, and probably experienced at turning away male attention.

As if to confirm his thoughts, a well-built, good-looking guy tried his luck with the mystery woman and was viciously shot down—weakling flea up against a fiery cannonball.

Still, Troy stayed, long after his drink was gone. She drew him, even in a spectator role. He wanted to be the fly on her wall and hang around, buzzing as long as she was here.

Red-Faced Guy decided he'd had enough and after a few weird comments, stumbled out, leaving only three empty seats between Troy and Womanhood Personified. Ludicrously, his heart started pounding. The bartender offered another arak, and though he'd been fine before, Troy felt exposed now, and answered yes. His peripheral vision caught the woman registering his presence. More than registering, she was watching him. His drink came, and in the act of pouring, he gave in to his impulse and turned to meet her eyes.

Boom.

He'd expected her to have an effect on him; hell, he'd practically gotten a hard-on watching her eat, but he hadn't expected…this. It was as if he'd lit up, as if every nerve ending in his body had come to life in a way he'd never felt before, ever, not even close. They heated up, uh, like a life, um, heat…

Uh-oh. He was in trouble.

She looked away, then back.

Boom. Again. Stronger this time. The rest of Justin's words sang in Troy's brain: *This is it. This is her. I just met the rest of my life.*

Jeez. *Get a grip.*

She looked away again and continued eating, not with her previous sexy immersion into the experience, each bite contemplated, taken, then savored, but robotically, unvaryingly, bites brought to her mouth, chewed, swallowed, repeated, as if she were seriously rattled. As if she'd just locked eyes with destiny and wasn't sure she liked what she saw. Unless Troy was simply projecting what he wanted her to be feeling.

He sipped his drink, sipped again, needing the courage more than the buzz. The last guy who tried to get on base with her struck out before the pitch was even completed. Troy could suffer the same fate no matter how intense their eye contact had been.

Or he could not.

Another sip, and he'd decided. "Nothing ventured, nothing gained," his father always said, usually before he was about to try a difficult golf shot, which he generally missed.

So…what to say?

Hi, I'm Troy.

Oh, was that clever.

Can I buy you a drink?

Zero points.

How about them Brewers?

Yeah, right.

You look like someone who really enjoys her food.

Hmm. That wasn't so bad.

Another check on his neighbor—she was gripping her glass, staring straight ahead, apparently unaware of his continued presence. *Hello? Little encouragement here?* Even a glance?

Apparently not.

One last sip of arak and he'd do it, no matter what.

Movement caught his eye and he found her this time with wallet in hand.

He took the last sip hastily. "Leaving?"

She stiffened as though the word had cornered her, then turned slowly. This time, though, Troy was prepared for the impact.

Boom.

No, he wasn't.

"Thought I might."

"Can I buy you another drink instead?" No, it wasn't original, but he was working under pressure.

She didn't answer. She barely moved. For someone who'd been so full of life when she walked in, casting her aura over the entire bar, she'd become oddly colorless and shut down.

He felt unaccountably protective of her, this older woman he knew absolutely nothing about, a woman who seemed more than able to take care of herself, and certainly more than able to answer a yes/no question about wanting a drink.

"No?" He held his breath.

She blinked, as if he'd disturbed some internal debate. Panic flitted over her features, which grew his confidence.

"Or…yes?" He suppressed a smile. Nice to know he had the ability to spark some kind of confused reaction in her. Because she'd done nothing but confuse the hell out of him since she made her entrance.

Miraculously, she put her wallet away, got down from the stool and sauntered toward him, hand held out for a shake. "Yes."

Yes.

He took her hand. The contact with her skin seemed intimate, familiar and right. He wanted to draw her into his arms and find her mouth. But since all she'd agreed to was a drink, that probably wasn't a great idea. "My name is—"

"No." She had a finger up to his lips fast enough to cut him off, startle him and make him want to close his mouth to taste her. "Don't tell me your name."

"Why, you want to guess?"

Her pretty brows drew together. "I don't want to know it."

"Why not?" Was she married?

"Female prerogative."

"Okay. Have a seat?" He gestured unnecessarily to the stool

next to him—she was already climbing on—and he caught her scent. Frying oil? Herbs? Roasted meat? She'd been in a kitchen somewhere.

"Would you like another arak?"

"Please."

He signaled the friendly, efficient bartender and pointed to Darcy; the man nodded and got down the bottle and a clean glass.

"Can you tell me *your* name?"

"No." The word came out as a simple statement of fact.

Troy regarded her with amusement. "So I guess asking what you do is out of the question, too?"

"Do we really need the details?"

"What's wrong with them?"

"Sometimes they get in the way."

"Of?"

"Of what we're both after." She was still speaking matter-of-factly, but he could sense high energy, see her fingers clenching and opening on her thighs.

"And what is that?"

"A night together. No strings."

He waited for his body to react, but the adrenaline rush was muted. Mystery Woman was acting as if this was a business transaction, though now that he was close, he could see that something vulnerable lurked under her facade of confidence. Her movements seemed less smooth than when she'd swept into the restaurant, her lips were held tighter. Did she really want to do this? "What makes you think a night together is what I want?"

"Your eyes told me."

She'd read that much right, though he hadn't been thinking one-night-no-strings as much as until-we-are-sick-of-each-other-or-die. "Are you married?"

"No." She spoke emphatically and he believed her. "Nor

seeing anyone. I'm just too busy to start a relationship, and prefer to keep entanglements to a minimum."

Apparently.

Troy didn't want limits, he wanted to dive in and explore her life and her mind, as well as her body. He still couldn't believe how powerfully he was drawn to her, how much this felt like something that had always been supposed to happen to him. As if he was welcoming it at last, like a much-anticipated reunion with a long-expected and familiar friend.

She tossed her hair back, exposing the flawless line of her long neck. He caught a light floral scent past the kitchen aromas, and his lips buzzed with the desire to touch and taste that skin.

"Are *you* married?" She eyed him suspiciously.

"No. Nor involved with anyone right now."

"Would you like to be involved with someone?" She leaned closer, inches away, eyes half-closed, lips curling up at the sides, begging to be kissed. The power of her nearness nearly blew him off his stool. "I mean right now. Right here?"

He hesitated before he accepted her invitation and met her lips. Something about this still felt surreal. Maybe that the attraction—and acting on it—was crazy, irresponsible, confusing, unlikely and very, very strong.

She pulled back nearly immediately from his kiss, as if it had startled her, then leaned in again, used her tongue to paint his lips, her teeth to nip, her mouth to smooth the bites.

Troy's cock responded, but his brain was asking for more than technique and teasing. It wanted a real kiss, one that joined them and took them over the way the mere meeting of their eyes had earlier.

He cupped the back of her head and kissed her the way he wanted, meeting her lips, moving lightly, then harder, not letting her back away from their erupting passion.

Her tongue tempted; he responded, and their touch heated

to the danger point. Too hot. He had to break free, hand still tangled in the hair at the nape of her neck, breath coming hard and fast.

This woman was serious trouble.

"Do you want to get out of here?" She was whispering, head bent, speaking to his chest.

His heart swelled with pleasure over what she was offering and caution over how easily the offer came. "You do this often?"

"No." She shook her head. "No."

"Why now?"

"Why not?"

That was no answer. There was more. He wanted at it. "Okay. Let's go."

"Where do you think we're going?"

"My place?"

"No." She looked up sharply. "Not mine, either. Hotel room."

He winced. He hadn't been in a hotel room with a woman since…ever. The one time he was, the girl hadn't been old enough to be classified as a woman. Prom night with a group of seniors. Couples took private turns in the room their parents thoughtfully paid for—though not for that purpose—while the rest hung out in the pool and game room areas.

"I just met you." She sat straight, pushing back hair that had tumbled forward. "I'm not letting you know where I live and I'm not going to your place. Hotel or nothing."

Troy narrowed his eyes. "Are you always this wide-open to negotiation?"

She shrugged. "In a hotel someone will hear me if I have to scream."

Her words chilled him, as did her casual attitude. Had she learned that lesson the hard way? He couldn't stand thinking about it. "You think I'm capable of hurting you?"

"No." She dropped her eyes. "But it's a mistake to rely entirely on instinct."

"I take it you've made that mistake."

"I did. Let's leave it at that."

Barriers again. He wanted to know everything about her, and she was apparently going to fight him every step of the way.

He threw down bills for the bartender and stood. Her eyes traveled quickly over him, top to bottom, and she must have liked what she saw, because her beautiful mouth curved into a smile. He escorted her outside into the still-chilly May air and over to her car. "I get to pick the hotel."

"Says who?"

"Me." Troy spoke firmly, saw her into the driver's seat. "The Pfister downtown. Meet me in the lobby."

He shut her door on her surprised face and walked to his car before she could collect herself enough to respond. If they had to make love in a hotel room, okay, but for his depraved trysts, Troy wasn't putting up with anything less than the best.

Roughly half an hour later, after a quick condom run, Troy met her in the Pfister's elegant lobby and traveled with her up to room 321.

"Home sweet home." He inserted the plastic card key and pushed open the door to the spacious, luxurious room done in rich shades of burgundy and gold: a bedroom with a four-poster king, a small sitting room and huge curtained windows that would have a view of Lake Michigan during the day.

"Nice. Beautiful, in fact." She walked in, tossed her purse on the bed, drew back the curtain to peer out the window, then let it fall and casually pulled her shirt over her head, exposing a black lace push-up bra supporting firm breasts, and a toned abdomen over the black pants sitting low on her hips. "Long day. I'm going to shower."

He stood watching her, taken aback, feeling almost super-fluous, erection pushing uncomfortably against the fly of his jeans while she lowered her pants and stepped out of them to reveal not more black lace, but thin pink cotton bikini underwear with faded red and purple hearts. The mismatch was oddly endearing.

"Want company in the shower?"

She shrugged as if she couldn't care either way. "Sure, if you'd like to."

If he'd *like* to? What was going on here? She was acting as if they were professional acquaintances, not two passionate people about to become lovers. Was she nervous or really this blasé about inviting strange men into bed? He didn't like either option. He wanted her hungry for him, excited, as anxious to touch and to discover him as he was to discover her.

Her hands disappeared behind her back; black lace came loose, uncovering round, high breasts with rose nipples that made Troy's mouth purse in anticipation of sucking. She wasn't looking at him, undressing as if he were a girlfriend she'd spent the day with and barely noticed in the room. The panties came down next in a matter-of-fact gesture, exposing closely trimmed dark hair through which peeked soft pink perfection.

Troy made a helpless sound between a groan and a moan. She either didn't hear or pretended not to know what she was doing to him, threw her panties on the bed and started to stride toward the shower.

He stepped deliberately in her way, pulling his shirt over his head. She was not turning their night together into an impersonal body-on-body encounter, and she was definitely not making it as far as the shower before he was inside her.

"Excuse me." Her eyes were wide searching his face, which must be reflecting his single-minded determination. "Could I please get to the shower?"

He pulled her against him, savoring the smoothness of her skin on his, and the lush pressure of her breasts. The lingering food odors had gone with her clothes; she smelled like woman and the subtle floral scent he'd caught earlier. "Shower later. You and me now."

"I don't think so."

"I do." He moved side to side, letting his chest brush her nipples, holding her eyes with his.

She shifted her gaze away, then back, put a hand to his sternum, but not forcefully. "I'm not clean. I'd rather—"

"You smell delicious. You smell like you." His voice came out a whisper; he kissed her bare shoulder, the base of her neck, her throat. "I want you now. Then shower if you have to, then I want you again. And again. And again."

He kissed her beautiful skin, longer between each word, undoing his jeans, pushing until they fell to his ankles and he could step out of them. Then he found her mouth, wrapped her tightly in his arms and lifted her, making her clutch at his shoulders and moan against his lips.

Yes. She wanted him, this stunning, incredibly hot, older and undoubtedly more experienced woman. She wasn't as indifferent as her methodical striptease suggested. His ego swelled along with his dick. He was going to make this good for her, good enough to break through that iron control. Maybe she'd tell him nothing about herself using words, but she'd tell him plenty with her body by the time this night was over. And in the days and nights ahead, he'd get to know the rest.

He toppled her back onto the mattress, which bounced them comfortably.

"Are you always this dictatorial?" Her breath was coming fast. She opened her legs to let him settle between them. He rubbed his erection against her beautiful sex through the thin cotton of his boxers.

"No, but I suspect you are."

"Always." She smiled up at him, dark eyes shining, hair splayed on the hotel pillow around her lovely face. Something shifted in his heart. What was it about this woman? He hadn't known her for more than a few hours.

"I bet you run something for your career." He touched his nose to hers, nuzzled her soft cheek. "Manage people. Boss crowds of them around."

"I told you, no personal details."

"No?" He rolled to the side, bringing her over with him, wondering what she was hiding from or scared of, and when or if she'd let him in. He trailed his fingers down her flat belly, forcing himself to go slower than he wanted, circled them in the short, soft hair between her legs, brushed her clitoris gently back and forth, loving the push of her hips in response. "How about *this* personal detail?"

"Oh." The syllable was soft, breathless. "You seem to know that one already."

"Mmm, yes." He teased her more, running his fingers slowly around her sex, exploring, reading her reactions—the thrust and grind of her hips, the catch in her breathing, the flutter of lashes against her cheek.

"And this?" Thumb rubbing a light circle on her clitoris, he slid a finger inside her, nearly going out of his mind with lust when her eyes shot open and a gasp escaped her.

"That *is* personal."

"Yes. It is." He pushed a second finger inside her, wanting to watch her come apart, to send her as far from the tightly controlled woman dispassionately pulling off her clothes as he could get her.

"Wait." She tried to squirm away from his fingers. "I'm... wait."

"No waiting." He bent and took her breast in his mouth, sucked the nipple, worshipped it with his tongue and teeth, kissed his way up to her throat, bit gently.

Her face flushed pink; she closed her eyes, panting help-lessly. "Wait."

"No," he said quietly. "Let it go, sweetheart, you're safe."

Her body went rigid; her eyes opened wide into his. Troy felt her muscles contract powerfully around his fingers, and practically lost it. He was dimly aware he had to remember the condom, but not much else registered except his need to be inside this woman as soon as possible.

Then he was, and she felt smooth and tight, gripped his cock perfectly, legs wrapped around him. In seconds, she was on fire all over again, hands working the muscles in his back, her hips bucking, face showing her pleasure, though she didn't meet his eyes. When he came, he had to keep from yelling, spasms of ecstasy shooting him impossibly higher, and then higher still after that.

She'd milked him dry, he was sure. Except in the shower he took her again, and again back on the bed, and once more in the middle of the night. In the morning, before his eyes were fully open, he reached eagerly for her, hard and ready to experience more of this insatiable woman for whom he was equally insatiable, who ruled his body and already at least part of his heart.

How could his life change so quickly? How could he go from so many pleasant, lukewarm dates with lovely women to an explosive all-night-long with someone who set him on fire with merely a look?

His hands met nothing on the other side of the bed; he rolled over and listened for her in the bathroom, wondering how he could have slept so deeply that he was entirely unaware of her getting up.

No sounds. He blinked, uneasiness creeping into his chest. She'd affected him more than any woman ever had, but the power in this situation was all on her side. He didn't know her name. He didn't have her number.

He threw off the covers, hurled himself out of bed. The sitting room was uninhabited; bathroom was dark, its door left ajar. He opened it anyway, sick with dread, flipped on the light and faced the inevitable emptiness of the room.

She was gone.

3

"CHAZ, THANKS FOR COMING IN today." Marie shook the strong, beautiful, masculine hand of strong, beautiful, masculine Chaz Hunter, and escorted his strong, beautiful, masculine body out of her office, barely closing the door behind him before she was pumping her fist. *"Yes!"*

This was the man for Darcy. Intelligent, articulate, funny, drop-dead gorgeous, built like an Olympic diver, divorced five years, didn't want kids and guess what he did for a living? Sold wine to stores and…wait for it…restaurants. He could not be more perfect. Marie could already envision long, sensual dates for the two of them spent tasting wine and food and each other. Chaz even loved the same kind of alternative rock music she did. Plus, from what Marie could tell, he came from money. So if Darcy ever needed a little cash infusion in her business, maybe to open a second location…

Okay. Marie was getting ahead of herself. But this guy was worth pulling out all the stops for, really attacking Darcy with how fabulous he was. And then when Darcy put her foot down and went mulish, as she very predictably and very annoyingly would, Marie could start thinking how to make this happen some other, less direct way. Some other, behind-the-scenes way. Some low-down, sinfully sneaky way.

Desperate times…

She pounced on her phone and dialed. Ten in the morning, Darcy wouldn't be at the restaurant yet, or if she was, she wouldn't be crazy busy and could talk. With any luck she'd even be able to listen.

"Darcy, it's Marie." She tried to keep the excitement out of her tone.

"Hey, what's up?"

"Not much." She sat back in her desk chair, grinning smugly. "Oh, except I just met your future husband."

"My—" Darcy groaned. "Well, isn't that fascinating, seeing as how I don't plan to get married ever."

"He's handsome, sexy, funny, sexy, rich, sexy—"

"Marie, what part of 'I don't want to date' doesn't get through your filter?"

"*And,* he sells wine to fine establishments such as yours. You'd have tons in common."

"We have one thing not in common right off the bat."

"You're female, he's male?" She laughed. "Honey, that's the best part. Or maybe you forgot."

"No-o. That's not i-i-t." Darcy sang the words as if she were taunting a sibling. "The difference is that he wants to date, and I *don't.*"

"You don't have to date. Just meet him."

"Oh, like that's going to—"

"Just look at his profile."

"Not interested."

"His picture."

"For heaven's—"

"How about listen to me saying his name?"

"*Marie!* You are a menace."

"Aren't I?" She was so enjoying this, twisting her chair side to side, sure she was finally on her way to victory, be it fair or foul. "You know I'm going to wear you down eventually. Why not give in?"

"Because." Darcy made a sound of frustration. "I don't need any more male complications right now."

Marie's chair stopped; her eyes shot wide. "*More* male complications? What do you mean 'more'? You met someone?"

"*No. No,* I didn't meet— For God's sake, Marie. You are obsessed. I think you need to see someone about this. A friend has a therapist who has helped her a lot with her complete and total insanity, yours can't be much worse. Or maybe it is."

"Chaz Hunter." She picked up a pen and wrote the name in the air with giant flourishes. "Chaz-z Hunter-r."

"*Chaz?* Oh, ew, what, his great-grandfather founded the Milwaukee Yacht Club?"

"His great-grandfather came over from Germany. They made money in construction. A lot of money."

"How nice for them."

"Just take a look." She suppressed a giggle, sensing Darcy was about to blow. "I'll send his picture to your—"

"Marie. I do not want—" A sharp thwack came across the line. Had a fish or chicken part just been severed while Darcy imagined Marie's head leaving her body? Silence, then a long suffering sigh. "Send it if you want, but I'm deleting upon receipt."

Excellent. She was weakening. Marie pulled up an email and attached Chaz's profile picture. "Darcy, in all seriousness, he seems like a really good guy. I can see you enjoying him a lot. And he's very hot."

"And therefore incredibly full of himself."

"Darcy, Darcy." Marie tsk-tsked. "You are horrifically sexist."

"I have to go. Delivery guy is here. Thanks for thinking of me, but I wish you wouldn't."

"Watch for his photo. Chaz Hunter." She hung up, sent the

email and let her head drop back, swinging the chair side to side again. Well. That was progress. Darcy's curiosity would undoubtedly prompt her to look at the picture, which was pretty fabulous. Chaz, standing on top of a spectacular mountain, clear blue eyes visible, strong chin shown to advantage, thick ashen hair ruffling sexily in the wind.

Sadly, Marie was pretty sure it would take a stronger push to get Darcy to talk to the guy even if she found his picture attractive. The first step would have to come from Chaz. But since Darcy didn't have a profile up on Milwaukeedates, Marie had nothing to show Chaz in order to interest him.

She stopped swinging the chair. Lifted her head. Stared at her laptop screen.

Now was the time.

Hadn't she recognized at the Women in Power meeting last week that she'd probably have to resort to fighting dirty in order to get Darcy to admit that love was what she deep down really wanted?

If Marie put up a Milwaukeedates profile for Darcy and steered Chaz in her direction, maybe he'd take it from there. What girl could resist being courted by a handsome, wealthy guy with loads of charisma and common interests? Certainly not Marie. If her friend Quinn, who met each one of those criterion, ever glanced romantically in her short, plump, average-woman direction, she'd melt into a gooey puddle.

There was always the chance, however, that Darcy, faced with the same irresistible combination, might freeze into a column of ice.

Marie's assistant buzzed. "Candy Graham on line three."

"Thanks, Jane." She connected the call eagerly. The perfect person to consult when hatching diabolical plans. "Hey, Candy."

"Marie, I had a completely fabulous idea."

"So did I." She grinned. Candy tackled everything with one hundred percent enthusiasm. "Let's hear yours first."

"You should have a party to celebrate all the Milwaukeedates couples who've gotten engaged or married through your site. Next month, June, is wedding month, the perfect time. I'm thinking end of the month, a wedding theme with tiered cake, flowers, champagne, maybe have a drawing for a donated certificate to a local bridal shop and/or tux rental place, or for the already-marrieds, to a kitchen or home improvement store."

"Wow. Wow!" Marie rose slowly from her chair as if helium was filling her. "What a great idea, Candy! Do we have time to plan a party in a month?"

"Are you kidding? Plenty. I'm happy to do it. I bet the paper would be willing to write up a piece on it, too. It'd be great PR for both of us. And I have friends at a couple of radio stations who might be willing to do interviews."

"Candy, you are brilliant." Marie started pacing her office, going back over the five years she'd been in business. "We've had about twenty-five couples engaged or married since we started, including you and Justin and Kim and Nathan."

"Fifty people is a perfect size. You can have it in your office, or…hey, maybe we can hold it at Gladiolas."

"Yes!" Marie was already picturing the dining room at Gladiolas decorated for a wedding theme. "I love it. Good PR for Darcy, too."

"Settled. So what was *your* completely fabulous idea?"

Marie gave a wicked grin. "Let's say I'm trying to extend your guest list by one more couple."

"Another set of lovebirds on the way?"

"I'm plotting. Darcy."

"Darcy?" Candy gave a shout of laughter. "You think you can get her *engaged* in the next month? I didn't think you could even get her interested in dating."

"I can't. But I'm still determined."

"How are you going to do it?"

"Er…" Marie wrinkled her nose. "I do have a plan, but it's not entirely ethical."

Candy hooted. "Are you going to have her put up four different profiles on Milwaukeedates the way you did with me?"

"One would be enough." She rubbed her temple, not entirely comfortable now that she'd have to admit to her scheme out loud. "The problem is that she refuses to consider it. So I was thinking maybe *I* could go online…"

"And put up a profile without her permission?"

Marie bit her lip anxiously. "It's horrible, isn't it."

"It is pretty horrible."

"I mean, it's really low."

"*Really* low."

"You don't think I should do it."

"Absolutely, I do." Candy sounded delighted. "It's perfect."

Marie snorted, wandering restlessly over to her bookcase. "I really don't know."

"C'mon, what's the worst that can happen?"

"She'd get angry with me."

"How does she feel about your matchmaking efforts on her behalf now?"

"Angry with me."

"Therefore…"

"I see your point." She ran a finger over the shelf. Needed dusting. "Except she could probably come after me legally. Invasion of privacy or something."

"Darcy wouldn't do that. Deep down she recognizes that as meddling and annoying as you are, Marie, you—"

"Oh, thanks. Tons."

"Sure, no problem. She realizes you love her and that's what motivates you. She wouldn't lash back at that. Not more than verbally."

"Which I would deserve." She went back to her desk and sank into the chair. Maybe this wasn't such a good idea.

"Which *we* would deserve. This is now officially *our* matchmaking plan. In fact, I'll call Kim and we'll make it a threesome idea."

"No, no. You shouldn't share blame with me."

"Who's talking blame? We'll want to share the *credit.* At her wedding."

Marie laughed. "You really think I should do this?"

"Absolutely. If nothing else it will get her attention. And any picture of her will definitely get the attention of men on the site. Then who knows? Once guys start flocking, she might just decide to give one or more of them a try."

"That was my hope." Marie logged onto Milwaukeedates as an administrator. "Okay, you're convincing me."

"We're convincing us. I'm going to call Kim right away. And listen, I'll do up an outline for the wedding party idea and email it to you by tomorrow or Monday, okay?"

"Love it. Thanks, Candy, on both counts. You're a gem."

"Aren't I? Seriously, I think forcing the issue with Darcy is a great idea. I saw her face when Kim was talking about wedding plans, and boy, look up *wistful* in the dictionary and there's her expression."

"Exactly." Marie was triumphant now. An enthusiastic ally had made all the difference.

"Speaking of her face, do you have a good picture of her? I might be able to dig one up."

"I doubt she can take a bad one." Marie brought up a New Profile page on her computer. "I have the photos I took at the Gladiolas opening. There's one in particular I remember as stunning."

"Awesome. That was a great dress she had on!"

"Okay, I'm on this. Thank you, Candy. Say hi to Justin."

"Say hi to Quinn."

Marie started, fingers stumbling over the keyboard. *Quinn?* "How did you know about him?"

Candy snickered. "Kim is my new gossip girl. She told me recently that she saw you two walking when she and Nathan were kayaking last month. Said you looked *aw*-fully happy."

"He's a friend. That's all." Marie was very glad Candy couldn't see her blushing.

"Uh-huh. Right. I believe that. One of these days we're all going to gang up on *you* for the matchmaking thing and see how you like it."

"Ooh, what a threat."

"You've been warned. Oh, and speaking of potentially good gossip, Wednesday night I saw Darcy heading for Esmee Restaurant. I'd just picked up Justin; he was drinking there with Troy. I tried to get Justin to ask if Troy had noticed Darcy—as if any man wouldn't—and if he noticed who she met up with, but you know men, their priorities are wacked, so Justin hasn't asked yet."

"Uh…okay." Marie's head was spinning trying to follow that one. "Wait, Darcy and Troy have never met?"

"Not as far as I know."

"Hmm." She narrowed her eyes, fingers tapping on the side of her keyboard. Troy. She hadn't thought of him for Darcy. Too young? Maybe not strong enough? "Let me know what you find out, especially if she's already got someone."

"You think she and Troy…?"

"I'm committing to nothing."

"Well, he's on the site, too, so you should definitely go ahead with our unethical plan. Oops, Justin's here. Talk to you soon!"

"Bye." Marie hung up, feeling slightly breathless, partly

from relief she'd dodged further questions about Quinn, and partly because she always felt that way after talking to her warm-hearted whirlwind of a friend.

Candy's party idea was terrific. Mid-June also brought Marie's fortieth birthday, something she wasn't quite sure she was ready to face. But celebrating the love she'd brought to so many couples would be a fitting way to show how rich her life had become and would continue to be.

For a second she imagined what richness her life would hold if Quinn was in it the way she'd come to realize she wanted him to be.

But that was ridiculous daydreaming. Marie had plenty more important things to do than fantasize about something she couldn't have. She opened her pictures file, searching for the photograph of Darcy she remembered best.

There. Darcy, caught unaware during a quiet moment at Gladiolas's opening, surveying her restaurant, color high, eyes sparkling, looking about as proud and happy and beautiful as any woman had a right to be.

The men of Milwaukeedates.com weren't going to know what hit them. And assuming Chaz reacted to her picture the way any sighted, intelligent, straight male would, Darcy wasn't going to, either.

"You did what?"

"Put up a profile for Darcy." Marie's smile slipped. Something was off tonight. From the moment she'd shown up at their usual Friday-night drink and dinner date here at the Roots Cellar bar in their shared neighborhood of Brewer's Hill, she and Quinn hadn't been able to settle into the usual easy camaraderie. She was used to him kidding about her matchmaking efforts, but while he usually reacted with amused exasperation, right now he seemed genuinely annoyed.

"And I sent Chaz a Milwaukeedates 'hello' supposedly from her, to get the ball rolling."

"This after she's said repeatedly that she doesn't want to date."

"Jeez, Quinn." She stared at him, getting annoyed herself, which was a first. She couldn't remember the two of them having anything but teasing, polite disagreements. Now Quinn wasn't teasing, and Marie didn't feel polite. "Haven't you listened to a thing I've told you about Darcy?"

"Sounds like you're not listening to a thing *she's* told you."

"She *does* want to date. You should see her talk about men."

"You mean hear her talk?"

"No, *see* her." Marie put down her Prufrock, her favorite Roots specialty drink, and turned on the bar stool, holding herself rigid. "Her whole body goes into terrified-defense mode, like this. Stiff as a board. She's so afraid to admit what she wants. So afraid someone will figure out she's human and can be vulnerable. It's heartbreaking."

"And up to you to fix?"

Grrrr. Even Quinn's strong resemblance to George Clooney wasn't helping her like him any better at the moment. "No, not up to me. Only she can fix it. But if I can put a guy in her way who will inspire her to take the necessary steps so she can ultimately be happy, then I've done something really wonderful for her."

He signaled the dark-eyed bartender, Joe, for another gin martini; he'd gone through his first one much faster than usual. "She'll be happy paired off because no one can be happy on his or her own? Is that what you believe?"

"Yes. I do believe that or I couldn't keep putting this much effort and time into what I do."

Quinn drained an invisible final drop from his empty drink

and pushed the glass away, then fixed his movie-star gaze on her. "And where do you fit into that, Marie?"

"What do you mean?" For some reason, maybe because his voice had gentled, Marie felt some of the fight leave her. "In my role as meddling matchmaker?"

"No. In your role as a woman. A single woman who shows no signs of wanting a man in her own life. Why is that? You don't want to be 'happy'?"

Irritation sparked again. "When it's time for me to date, I will."

"And when will that time be?"

When she could give up hope that Quinn might someday open his eyes and see her. "You want an exact hour?"

"Yes. I do."

"Okay, fine." She closed her eyes, took a deep breath. They were squabbling like children. This wasn't what she wanted. But maybe he was pushing her toward something she should be doing anyway. Setting a deadline. Deciding when to give up this pipe dream. "June 23 at 5:03 p.m."

He blinked. "How precise."

"The exact day and time I turn forty."

"I see." He turned the second drink Joe had brought him in a circle, as if deciding the angle at which to attack, raised the glass halfway to his mouth, then set it down. "So you're officially on the market as of then."

"Yes." Marie nodded firmly. No, she hadn't planned to draw that line, but having done so felt like the right and smart thing to do. By that night, newly forty-year-old Marie would either have summoned her courage to confess her feelings to Quinn, or decided there was no point and it was time to move on. Hanging on like this was only going to get harder and harder.

"And then you'll, what, sign up with a competitor's dating website?"

"I...guess so." She smiled at him, sick to her toes. How could she even think about dating anyone else feeling this way about Quinn? Obvious answer: she'd have to. "Or I'll ask friends if they know of anyone. Do you know of anyone?"

He did drink this time, a substantial gulp. "As a matter of fact, yes."

"Tell me about him."

"What do you want to know?"

"Well, is he handsome?" She didn't care. This was torture.

"Hmm. I'm not the one to ask about that, Marie. He's not my type."

"Fun to be with?"

"Yeah, I'd say he's pretty fun."

Somehow she kept smiling with a mouth that felt weighted. "Intelligent?"

"He is."

"In decent shape?"

"Sure."

"Revoltingly wealthy, I hope?" Like she cared...

"As a matter of fact, yes."

Marie scowled comically. "There must be something horribly wrong with him."

"Huh?" He gave her a sidelong look. "Why do you say that?"

"Well, obviously, if he's that perfect and not seeing anyone there's some ghastly defect you haven't figured out yet."

Quinn chuckled without humor. "Oh, you cynic."

"Me? I'm not the one dating a parade of women young enough to be my daughters." She meant to tease, but bitterness showed through. A lot of bitterness. Bitterness that belonged to her ex-husband and his child-bride, not to Quinn, who'd suffered through a betrayal of his own when his wife left him for another man.

Quinn's face darkened. "I gave up that chase, I told you."

Marie gathered herself together. Enough. This was horrible, and getting them nowhere.

"Quinn, something isn't right tonight. We seem unable to do anything but bicker."

He straightened his broad shoulders, rubbing the back of his neck. "You're right. Sorry. I'm on edge tonight."

"Work?" She wondered if something was going wrong with one of the companies he'd invested in. Though he didn't strike her as the type who'd risk more than he could comfortably afford to lose.

"Sort of." He frowned, staring into his gin. "There's a situation I've been counting on working out, and I'm starting to wonder if I've been reading it wrong. It's not like me."

"I'm sorry."

"I've invested a lot. Time, energy, emotion."

"Quinn." She leaned toward him, heart melting at his distress, put her hand on his forearm and squeezed the strong muscle reassuringly. "Is there anything I can do?"

"Yes, actually." He took another too-large sip of his martini. "Come to dinner with me at Dream Dance Steakhouse."

Marie's jaw dropped. The restaurant was one of Milwaukee's finest, and one of its most expensive. Not exactly a buddy date. "Wow. That's…a little out of my—"

"I'm inviting you. My treat. We can go dancing afterward."

League was how she'd been going to finish her sentence. Now she wasn't sure she was hearing correctly. "Dancing."

"Swing dancing at the Jazz House. If you'd enjoy that."

If? Was she dreaming? Quinn Peters, god among men, was inviting peasant-stock Marie on what sounded like a real manwoman date? She ducked her head to avoid showing her blush and took a solid breath so her voice would come out casually. "That sounds fun. When were you thinking of going?"

"Next Friday? Our regular night?"

"Sure." She was dreaming. If an operator like Quinn wanted her, he would have made that clear on their first meeting. Right? God, this was confusing. She reached instinctively for her drink, suddenly as thirsty for alcohol as he seemed to have been all night, took a big clumsy slug and started coughing.

"You all right?" He thumped her firmly on the back, a big brother's touch. He *had* told her months ago that she reminded him of his sister. Marie had been so humiliated, she'd invented a brother he could remind her of, too. Only he hadn't looked humiliated at all at the comparison.

"Fine. I'm fine." She wiped her streaming eyes. "Just haven't learned how to swallow yet."

"You might want to try." His hand lingered briefly between her shoulder blades, then slid slowly down her spine before he finally broke the contact.

Not quite a lover's touch, but not a brother's, either.

Marie reacted as if he'd kissed her, desire running hot for more of the same. *Help.*

Next Friday. Dinner and dancing. She'd be in his arms out on the floor, possibly held close against him. If a pat on the back got her this heated, she'd end that night up in flames.

Still without knowing whether this man she burned for had any interest in putting them out.

4

"CHEF?" ACE KNOCKED ON THE door to Darcy's cramped enclosure—which she optimistically called her "office"—in the back of Gladiolas's kitchen. "We have a problem with this morning's delivery."

Darcy turned her chair away from the computer where she'd carefully saved a new recipe into her Chef's Bible file: one copy there, password protected, and one on the red flash drive she kept hidden in a drawer. The file was sacred; in it she kept all her food creations, past present and future, and all her ideas for Gladiolas's specials. This was a menu she called Save Calories for Dessert, which featured local bass steamed over a fragrant curried broth, served alongside roasted zucchini and couscous studded with raisins and almonds. A light salad of avocado, grapefruit and endive, and then a killer dessert with layers of white milk and dark chocolate mousses in a bitter chocolate shell.

"A problem? Oh, goody." She took in Ace's unruly red hair and bloodshot eyes. The kid showed promise, but he'd never get anywhere smoking it away 24/7. Half of her wanted to talk to him, to guide him toward the straight and narrow, the way her mentor, Chef Paul, had guided her. The other half told her it was none of her business what he did with his life and career. "What is it?"

Ace held up a bundle of green stalks. "Celery instead of celeriac."

Darcy brought forth her favorite word. *She* didn't have a problem exhibiting basic competency, why did the rest of the world? "Send it back. I'll call Ken."

"Yes, boss." Through the window surveying the kitchen, which she'd heard staff refer to as "big brother," she watched Ace amble away, playing catch with the celery. The kid could take just about any hit the business gave out and barely blink. During more than one crazy, pressured shift he'd saved their butts by calmly stepping onto the line and taking up the slack when orders got ahead of them. He also got the job checking in deliveries because he was smart as hell, even stoned, and Darcy trusted him above anyone else in the kitchen. Even her sous chef Sean, who did what he was told, but didn't contribute much else.

She dialed the Lenson's sales rep, still fuming. Darcy did not take on problems with barely a blink. Maybe she should try some of Ace's weed. "Ken, it's Darcy. Doug showed up with a crate of celery. I ordered celeriac. I'll need the right stuff here ASAP. Like now."

"Celeriac…" His voice was doubtful.

"I don't care where you have to get it, just get it. I can't serve mashed celery. Andy Gerber was nosing around here the other day and I can tell you, his pricing is nice. And he's cuter than you."

"I'll find it," Ken said immediately. "I'll have it there in under two hours."

"I'll hold you to that." She hung up, imagining Ken indulging in choice vocabulary at her expense. Whatever. If you didn't keep the pressure on, people bled out from ineptitude.

She emerged into the kitchen, took a quick glance around. "Where the hell is my sous chef?"

"Dunno." Ace poked his head out of the cooler, arms full of asparagus. "I'm sure he'll be here any minute."

"Can you start the dinner prep if he's not here in five?" Sean wasn't usually late, but apparently today he was joining the Drive Darcy Nuts Club.

"Sure." He looked at her curiously. "You're off today, chef. You aura is all out of whack. What's up?"

Darcy glared at him. "My *aura* is fine. Have Sean come see me when he gets in."

She stomped back to her office. Yes, her aura was off today. Everything was off today. Sean had gone missing, tonight's featured side dish was in jeopardy, the kid she'd like to move up onto the line was stoned 24/7, Marie was being particularly pigheaded...and Darcy could not stop thinking about *him*.

She wasn't proud of her sexual history—she wasn't ashamed, either—but since she'd given up on relationships after Chris, her postcollege boyfriend, cheated on her with a woman who had no life outside of catering to him, Darcy had been with enough men to know that once they were out of her bed and she was back in her kitchen, it was all about the work, her true passion. In a quiet moment she might let her thoughts drift briefly, maybe get a quick smile or shot of arousal out of a particular memory of a lover. But she'd never had her brain hijacked to this extent, as if she'd imprinted on the guy. His body, the way he touched her, his voice, the way he touched her, his scent, the way he'd touched her...

He touched her as if every inch of her body deserved exploration and adoration. His hands were never still—brushing lightly, bringing nerve endings to life, warming her with smooth, sensuous stroking or kneading deeply to soothe tired muscles. She knew herself around men; she had definite limits. She got antsy under sustained physical caresses and she couldn't sleep in contact with a male body.

That night? She'd loved this man's hands on her, had stretched and grinned and purred like a cat in silent ecstasy. Afterward, wrapped in unfamiliar arms in a strange hotel room, she'd slept like a rock. Did this make sense? No. Worse, at dawn, she'd slipped out of the warm, comfortable bed to use the bathroom and returned with the assumption that her right-now man would be awake and ready for another round. But he'd slept on peacefully, his big, lean body sprawled under the sheet. The sight of that dark tousled head on the white pillow, lashes black against his cheek, stubble shadowing his strong chin... Darcy had succumbed to an overwhelming wave of tenderness that had made a mockery of all the vague, empty feelings she'd experienced on other mornings-after, and which had left her literally breathless. And scared.

What did Darcy do when she was scared? She shut down and she ran. The way she did when Dad went into his drunken rages. The way she did when boyfriends betrayed or hurt her. Reflexive flight, an animal-deep instinct for self-preservation. This time, though, she was flying away from something that felt more dangerous than rage or abuse. Something she couldn't define beyond certainty that it had threatened to devour her whole.

She only had herself to blame. Three nights ago at Esmee Restaurant, after she'd locked eyes with her recent lover, but before he'd spoken to her, she could have listened to the instinct telling her to leave. Even after he started a conversation, she should have left, knowing she was at a low point that night, vulnerable and lonely, and knowing better than to think men were any kind of answer to what ailed her. Hadn't she been screeching that exact lecture at Marie for months now? But the chemical connection between them had been so powerful...

Yeah, well, Darcy had gotten all the trouble she'd gone looking for and more.

Her office phone rang, startling her back to real life. "Gladiolas, this is Chef Darcy Clark."

"Hey there, honey."

Oh, hurray. The day was getting worse and worse. "Raoul. What do you want?"

"You." His playful, deep voice did nothing for her. She cringed that she'd ever found him attractive. He had that dark, tattooed, ponytailed, muscled bad-boy thing going, which she generally found irresistible. But there was bad boy and there was slime-boy, and he'd crossed the line. "I miss ya, Darce."

"Uh-huh. Why are you calling?"

"Can't a friend call to check on you?"

"Yes, of course." She put a big smile in her voice. "Of course a friend can. It's just that you're not one."

"Oh, sweetheart. You've gotta let that anger go before it eats you up."

"I will *so* keep that in mind." She wanted to growl at him. "Once more, why are you calling?"

"I *told* you. I miss you, I miss the old place. I was wondering if you'd like to get together."

"For?" What did he want? Why was he doing this? She instinctively closed her latest Chef's Bible document. Not that he could see into it over the phone, but she didn't trust the guy for a second, and if her recipes got into his hands, he'd no doubt make full use of them. Excellent technician in the kitchen, zero on creativity.

"A talk."

"About?"

"Jeez, you are a tough one. A talk about anything. About you, about how you're doing, about how Gladiolas is doing. Two professionals shooting the breeze about the biz."

"And about your suspiciously familiar-sounding new venture?"

"Babe…"

"Name is Darcy. Use it. And sorry, no time for a drink, I'm busy."

"That's definitely my loss." His voice dropped into the seductive tone that had actually tempted her before she found out he was sleeping with Alice, their only married waitress. Before she found out boxes of steaks and pounds of expensive cheeses were disappearing into his truck. "Any men in your life?"

"Hundreds. Can't keep track of them all. I have to go now."

"So when's a good time for our date?"

"Oh, gosh, let me see." Darcy paused as if consulting her calendar. "How about next…never?"

"Look, Darce…"

"Darcy."

"Darcy. We're both in this business now. I don't see anything wrong with forming an alliance. We can both benefit from—"

"You go your way. I'll go mine." She whacked her forehead with her palm. "Oh, wait, sorry, I got that wrong. I meant, I go my way. You copy me."

"Hey. That's not—"

She hung up, more rattled than she'd ever let him know. He reminded her of a jerk she knew in college who kept suggesting he and Darcy study together, which meant he wanted her to summarize the course material so he could avoid preparing for exams himself.

Instinct told her she was hanging on in this city only by being unique, and if Raoul's new venture took off in its better location with her menu style and format, he could sink Gladiolas and her with it. The perfect way to get ahead for someone with no special talent, and the perfect revenge on her for having fired him.

Was it time to go to bed yet? She'd never sleep with all this fear and fury inside her, though. Sometimes she did worry that her anger would eat her up. Or that her emotions would explode and she'd fly off, fragmented, into the ether. She needed ballast in her life, some emotional constancy that would give her what she—

Oh, no. No.

Darcy covered her face with her hands and leaned on her desk. Would she never learn? Ballast…emotional constancy…

She'd immediately gone back to thinking about *him*.

TROY HAULED HIMSELF OUT OF THE Milwaukee Athletic Club's pool, breathing hard. Seventy laps had been all he could handle today. He'd done a sloppy, unfocused job, his concentration shot. Didn't do much better at work that day, either. Half-assed, in fact—luckily it wasn't a crunch week. And thank God he wasn't still designing interactive webpages for the book with Justin on top of his day job. That would have gotten exactly nowhere.

He stood, dashing water out of his hair, and headed for his towel.

"Hi there."

Troy turned at the familiar voice. Oh, man. He'd forgotten about Missy. More proof of how far he'd fallen from sanity. "Hey, how's it going?"

"Great." She dimpled a sweet smile. "You looked sharp out there."

"Actually, it felt bad today. Just didn't have it."

Missy nodded sympathetically, water darkening the blond strands of her short hair, droplets glinting on her cheeks. She didn't bother to hide that she was doing her usual thorough check of his body. "Those days suck. You heading to the weight room now?"

"Uh…" Did she have his routine memorized? He'd noticed Missy over a month ago—her stunningly toned body and pretty features were hard to ignore. Since then he'd intersected with her here at the pool or on the machines a few times a week, more often recently. They'd struck up a casual friendship, talking mostly about their workouts. Troy had been flattered by the attention, and before the night at Esmee, he'd been planning to ask Missy out, to see if his initial interest could grow into anything more.

Now, faced with the same person he'd been fantasizing about less than a week ago, he hadn't the slightest idea what had seemed special about her. Well…maybe the slightest idea. Her body was in great shape. But today, instead of flawless, it looked overmuscled. She was very attractive, yes, but she didn't have the kind of beauty that hollowed him out with a glance.

In short, Missy wasn't *her*. She who still had him hollowed out, in spite of the fact that she hadn't been interested in anything but screwing him and getting the hell away.

"I'm meeting friends for a beer later. Going to skip the weights today." He hadn't been planning to meet friends or skip the weights, but he wasn't in the mood to listen to Missy's cheerful chatter. He could still lift at home.

"Oh, too bad." She sidled closer, tipped her head to look up at him coyly. "Listen, I was wondering…"

His body tensed. Back a few days, he would have been eager to hear whatever she was about to say. Now every instinct was telling him to make his escape.

"If you'd like to have a drink together sometime?"

There it was. The invitation he'd been planning to extend. He should go out with her. He had no reason to think The Woman wanted to see him again, or that she'd be able to find him even if she did. Troy wasn't quite pathetic enough to sit hopefully at Esmee every night until she happened in again, though he was so taken with her it had crossed his mind.

Going out with Missy was a good idea. An excellent way to loosen the unfortunate vise grip this unnamed lover had his brain and balls in.

He opened his mouth to accept, but at the last millisecond his brain did an about-face without his permission. "Thanks, Missy, but I've just started dating someone and want to see where that goes."

What the hell had he just said?

"Ah. Okay. I completely understand." She pasted a smile back on her disappointed face and nudged him with her hard shoulder. "Let me know if it doesn't work out, though, okay?"

He grinned, feeling like a lying piece of dirt. "Absolutely. Thanks again for the invite."

"Sure." She gave a sexy little wave and walked toward the women's locker room, her virtually fat-free ass swinging invitingly.

What kind of idiot was he? She was a nice woman, seemed levelheaded and even-tempered, far from making the scenes Debby loved or playing his recent lover's frustrating mind games. At very least they could have had a pleasant evening. By clinging to his fantasy of wild, lifelong passion, he risked setting himself up for a lifetime of hurt and alone, and a lifetime of hurt and alone didn't appeal to him.

Except…how could he force himself to be eager giving someone routinely attractive to him a chance now that he knew it was possible to catch fire from a first glance?

He trudged to the locker room, showered, dressed and drove slowly home to Whitefish Bay, dragged himself inside his house, dragged into the kitchen to feed Dylan, who followed him around, tail wagging sympathetically. Dragged himself

into a chair to stuff food down his throat. Dragged himself
to the living room to find nothing he wanted to watch on TV.
Dragged himself into his bedroom to be completely uninterested in a vastly complicated murder mystery novel.

C'mon, man. Troy was acting like a lovesick teenager. So
he couldn't have That Woman. There were others. Single ones,
desirable ones. He was paying to be part of the Milwaukeedates site so he could find those women easily. Sitting here
moping was bull crap.

He fired up his computer, logged on to Milwaukeedates.com.
*Man, twenty-six, seeking woman, twenty-three to thirty-three,
within fifty miles of Whitefish Bay, Wisconsin. No smoking.
Pictures only.* Go.

The list came up, thumbnail photos with member-chosen
nicknames and a few bits of basic information next to each.
He'd already seen most of the profiles on the first page, so
he clicked an icon to re-sort the list so the latest subscribers
would show first.

The machine did its work; the list reappeared.

At the first picture, a woman who called herself Foodie101,
Troy did a double take, then stared, mouth hanging open in a
cliché of astonishment.

Her. What the hell?

Emotion punched him in the solar plexus, and it wasn't
pretty. He'd been trying to console himself with reasons she
might have run, telling himself she was a free agent, not out
for any kind of entanglement, uninterested in more than one
night with a man. That it wasn't him, it was her.

When that didn't do much to quell his obsession, he'd told
himself what they had was special, and maybe even though
she'd panicked initially, eventually she'd move heaven and
earth to find him again, because there was no way anyone
could squander the chance to explore a connection so instan-
taneous and so powerful.

All of that sounded good, and he'd clung to it. Until now. Because here she was, the woman who'd wanted to avoid even exchanging names, right there in a public forum trying to find the love of her life.

So it wasn't a matter of her not wanting a man, not wanting a relationship, not wanting more than one night.

It was a matter of her not wanting *him*.

DARCY FLIPPED ON THE LIGHT AND stood for a moment, surveying her neat entranceway and small living room beyond. It was later than she usually got home. She'd been reluctant to leave Gladiolas, kept making excuses to stay, until the staff was ready to throw her out. Usually, her cozy matchbox of a ranch house in the working-class Milwaukee neighborhood of Washington Heights represented peaceful sanctuary, a place to relax, do a yoga or another of her workout tapes, let her mind wander over a cup of coffee, thinking of ingredients, flavors and techniques she could combine into a new recipe and a new page for her Chef Bible file.

Tonight, in the bone-chilliness of early June, restlessness had followed her home.

Shivering, she kicked off the black flats she kept in her office at Gladiolas to change into, since the shoes she wore in the restaurant kitchen were unspeakably dirty by the end of the evening. Down the hall to her bathroom, she stripped and immersed herself in the brisk, efficient shower she'd gotten down to a water-conserving, three-minute science, emerging refreshed and relieved of the overload of kitchen odors.

After such a crappy start to the day with her sous chef late and the delivery mix-up, the afternoon and evening had gone fine. Ken had shown up apologetically—at the last possible second—with enough celeriac to satisfy her and the diners who'd ordered it. The special—Fishing for Compliments— trout with roasted artichokes and pecans had been a hit. Right now she was supposed to be working out more summer specials, thinking sunshine, hot weather and long, lazy days on the beach.

Dressed in her favorite nightgown—full-length soft cream flannel trimmed with blue—and its matching blue fleece robe, which she'd generally put away by this time of year, she started the coffee and visited her chocolate stash for three Hershey's Special Dark miniatures. Less than three wasn't enough. More than three and she risked inviting a binge like the ones she used to have after a night of excessive partying, when her sugar-craving body would demand a whole bag.

Those days were behind her, stopped by her beloved late boss and mentor, Chef Paul, at the restaurant Gold Bistro where she got her start. He'd casually let drop one evening that if she wanted to stay a dishwasher, coming in to work drunk would be fine, but if she wanted to become a chef, she better cut out that behavior immediately. Since Darcy had only given fantasy time to that dream in her most secret heart of hearts, she'd been shocked into silence. And sobriety. Good thing, because with the alcoholic gene in her family, she could easily have landed herself in serious trouble like her sister, Brit, now nearly a decade into recovery.

Shortly after that conversation, Chef Paul had given her a thrilling tryout on the kitchen line, then followed that test with a promise that if she kept her grades up in high school, he could see about recommending her for a scholarship to the hospitality program at the University of Wisconsin. From then on, her life had direction and meaning, and she'd blossomed so far beyond where she thought she'd end up that she still had to pinch herself sometimes.

Before Chef Paul, no one had ever treated her as if she had the potential to be anything but a pain in the ass, a reputation that she'd done her very best to live up to. When he died, she'd grieved more for him than the loss of anyone or anything else, before or since.

Decaf brewed, she poured herself a cup and took it over to her laptop, set by the kitchen window with a view of her minuscule backyard—fifteen minutes to rake or mow. One by one her friends had paired off and moved farther out to bigger yards and houses that would hold their growing families. That life wasn't for her. She loved living in the city, loved her private rhythms and space, loved to feel the beat of humanity right outside her walls.

Her email program opened and loaded new messages; she scanned the list. The first was the forwarded profile from Marie, which she deleted unopened as she promised herself, though admittedly she did have a twinge of curiosity. One from Brit, one from a guy she used to work with, one from…who was this? Hunterman@Milwaukeedates.com. Hunterman? Below that, another. From TallGuy@Milwaukeedates.com.

Spam? These weren't from Marie, but had someone hacked Marie's site and generated crap mail using a stolen address book?

Darcy opened the first email. The picture of a guy leaped out at her, model-handsome, caught by the camera in a ridiculous top-of-the-mountain, look-how-rugged-I-am pose.

Hi there. Thanks for the 'hello,' I'm glad you found me. I'm interested right back atcha. You are very good-looking and obviously articulate and intelligent. I'm a wine salesman, and would love to tell you more about what I do over a glass of fine Merlot. Or if you'd rather keep it to email for now, tell me about yourself. I'd love to know more.

Look forward to hearing from you.

Chaz.

Chaz? Chaz as in, *Ew, his grandfather probably founded the Milwaukee Yacht Club?* The guy Marie was trying to shove down Darcy's throat? What the hell was he talking about? Thanks for what, "hello"? What made him think she was articulate and/or intelligent?

How did he get her email address?

Marie? No, no way. Marie liked to meddle, but even she wouldn't stoop to something that invasive and obnoxious.

But then…who was this other person?

She opened the second email from TallGuy; her heart started pounding violently at the same time the rest of her froze solid.

Him. The picture was unmistakable, and even looking into a digital replica of his eyes Darcy felt that crazy burst of energy.

I want to see you again.

Thrills. An amusement park ride of them roller coastering all over her body.

I want to see you again. That was it. Short and sweet. Not asking permission, not begging, not apologizing, not negotiating. Stating a want. Leaving it at that. Hers to do with as she chose.

Oh, my lord.

Her in-box notifier chimed, startling her back to the real world and this bizarre email intrusion. She gasped and put a hand to her temple. What was this? Another *three* emails from Milwaukeedates. Three introductory "hellos" from three more guys. It was almost as if she were signed up on the site, and men were able to find her and—

No. *No way.*

She shoved her chair back from the table, pounced on her phone and dialed, not caring what time Marie went to bed or what might be a decent or polite hour to call.

"Hey, Darcy, what's—"

"Why the hell am I getting emails from Milwaukeedates.com guys? Specifically from Chaz, who you were just trying to fix me up with, but also this other person, TallGuy."

"Troy?" Marie gasped. "*Troy* wrote to you?"

Something turned ice-cold in Darcy's chest. "Troy?"

"Justin and Candy's friend. He signed up months ago, in February. I guess he found your profile. I was only going to leave it up a while longer, to make sure Chaz—"

"That guy, TallGuy, is *Justin and Candy's friend Troy?*"

"Yes." She sounded surprised, undoubtedly by Darcy's incredulous and slightly hysterical reaction. "That's him. Isn't he gorgeous? Get now why Candy always fans herself when she talks about him?"

"Yeah. Um, I guess." She could barely think, barely get her mouth to form coherent words. In some sickening coincidence, she'd unwittingly slept with someone her friends all knew. If they found out, the matchmaking would be relentless.

So. They wouldn't find out. She wouldn't see him again, and that would be that. As long as he didn't find out who she was…

"Why?" Marie's voice sharpened into curiosity. "Do you know him?"

"Of course not. Of course I don't." Darcy sank back into her chair. Troy's eyes were still smiling at her from her laptop; she couldn't stand looking at them, and couldn't stand looking away. "Marie? Why do I have a profile up on Milwaukeedates?"

"Gloves are off. I'm playing dirty now," Marie said cheerfully. "I want you to stop shutting your life off from possibilities. Meet men like Chaz and Troy, fall in love and live happily ever after as people are meant to do."

"Not all people." Darcy jumped out of her chair. "My parents? Not happily and didn't last ever after. Neither did my—"

"You don't have to have your parents' relationship. In fact, you have every reason not to."

"It's not just them. I have my career to think of now, and

Gladiolas. What guy is going to put up with the hours I keep?"

"You can have a career and love, too, Darcy. Millions of women do it, and millions of men support them."

"Good for them." She clutched her head, trying to control a scream rising up through her body. "But I guarantee those women are still doing the lion's share of the work at home. I'm hardly ever home to begin with. You should have seen my father when he got laid off and Mom had to work and couldn't cater to him anymore. You should have seen my boyfriends when—"

"Not all men are like that."

"All the ones I fall for are. It's a cycle and I can't break it."

"Maybe a therapist…"

"I don't have time for that, either."

Marie gave a long-suffering sigh, which made Darcy want to pinch her. "Candy, Kim and I can all see how much you want this."

"*They're* in on this, too?" She wanted to cry at the betrayal.

"We understand that you're scared, that you have every reason to think you can't be happy. Candy and Kim just went through similar journeys and look how happy they are now. All we're doing is nudging you in the direction you deep down already want to go."

"*I* want to go?" Anger upgraded to rage, which Darcy was uncomfortably aware contained some of the exact fear Marie was talking about, plus panic that once again people she thought she could trust weren't worthy of that gift. "So the three of you have ganged up and decided you know more about me than I do."

"We're with you, not against you."

"*And* the three of you think Mr. Big-Chin-on-a-Mountain is going to make me a real woman?"

"You're already a real woman. We want you to be a real happy woman. If not Chaz, then someone else. Maybe Troy? He's obviously interested in you if he wrote. All of us who have met him can vouch for what a great guy he is. Candy's brother has been friends with him for a long time. And Justin—"

"I cannot do that again." Her voice broke.

"Again? Troy?" Marie's voice grew softer. "Does this have anything to do with that 'male complication' you were talking about the other day, Darcy?"

"*No.*" Her voice showed the strain. "Not 'again' with Troy, I meant I can't do that again with men in general."

"How did you like Esmee the other night?"

Darcy stiffened. *She couldn't know.* "You three have me under surveillance?"

Marie chuckled. "Candy was pretty sure she saw you heading inside when she was there picking up Justin, who'd just left Troy at the bar. Maybe you saw him there without realizing who he was?"

Darcy closed her eyes. She could lie, but Candy would ask Justin, and Justin would ask Troy and who knew what he'd say?

"I had a drink with a guy. That was it." Her voice had risen and thinned. She sounded exactly like the liar she was. "I didn't know who he was. We didn't exchange names."

"No names? One drink? That was it?" Marie's sweet voice was coaxing now.

"No, Marie, we went straight to a hotel afterward and had sex all night long." She pulled off the sarcasm, but her hearty laugh faked for good measure fell absolutely flat. *Shut up, Darcy. Just shut up.* She'd done exactly what her sister's three-year-old did. *Mo-o-m, I didn't just take a crayon and write all over the walls in the living room.* "Isn't that all in your spy report?"

"No spies, Darcy." The gentle reproach brought Darcy near tears. Damn it. She didn't want to feel this way. She didn't want this to have happened to her just when she was feeling so strong and independent and untouchable. And she didn't want friends who cared about her so much they made complete pains of themselves and threatened her well-being.

"Please leave me alone, Marie, all of you. This is my life, and it's up to me how I live it."

She hung up the phone, walked down the hall to her perfectly organized room, took one look at the flawlessly made empty queen bed and burst into painful tears.

5

TROY THREW DYLAN'S RUBBER BONE once again across his living room and into the kitchen. Dylan's compact golden body raced after it; he ended its life fiercely for the umpteenth time with growls and head-shaking, then brought his prize proudly back to Troy. Who threw it again. And again. Bonding, exercise and a way to pass the endless ticking seconds.

After Troy had sent a short, simple email to "Foodie101," he'd gone into his exercise room, headed straight for his weights and worked the hell out of his body. Exhausted, he'd showered, pulled on sweats, made himself something to eat, and only then allowed himself to check for a response.

None. Okay, too soon.

For two hours he'd watched a terrible TV movie about a single mom trying to stop gang wars in her neighborhood. Then checked email again.

Still no response, but using the Milwaukeedates.com software, he'd been able to see that she'd read his note.

Some progress. And increased restlessness. And hope. And dread.

Now, roughly twenty minutes later, he was still waiting for her reply. Or for her nonreply. With luck she'd put him out of his misery soon with a clear response. *Yes, I'd like to see you again,* or, *No, I'd rather eat bugs.*

Dylan bounded back from the kitchen, feathery tail wagging, red bone clenched in his mouth, which was surrounded by white fur, the only deviation from gold except for a few flecks of white on his ears that looked like splattered paint. Troy extracted the toy and threw it again. That time it didn't make the kitchen, but bounced off the doorway and tumbled back onto the floor, landing only a few yards from where Troy was sitting. Dylan still pounced with furious excitement. Wouldn't that be nice, when life events fell way short of expectations, to be so thrilled anyway? People could learn a lot from dogs.

So. Troy glanced toward his laptop, sitting tantalizingly close on his coffee table. Too soon to recheck email? Probably. He sent the bone out again. And again. And again, until even Dylan's fervor seemed to be waning. He let the dog keep his now-sodden toy, got himself a beer and crossed once more to his laptop. Many more times and he'd wear a path in the carpet.

Still nothing. Jeez, she could take days to answer or not answer at all. Troy needed to put it and her out of his mind.

But before he did that, he wanted one more peek at her profile picture, wearing that slinky blue dress, poised and confident, eyes snapping brilliantly. He'd gotten hard just looking at her, remembering that same flush on her face right before she surrendered to the orgasm tearing through her.

He clicked on her profile link, his body responding already to the memory. Why was he torturing himself like this?

The link didn't go through. *Profile not found.*

He tried it again. Nothing.

On the Search page of Milwaukeedates.com, he typed in her handle, Foodie101.

Nothing. He hadn't misspelled it, he was sure.

He tried the general search, the way he'd found her the first time. *Man seeking women, twenty-three to thirty-three, within fifty miles of Whitefish Bay, Wisconsin. No smoking, pictures only. Go.*

The list came up. He sorted it to put the most recent profiles first.

Nothing.

She was gone.

What the hell? If he didn't still have his email to her Milwaukeedates nickname in his Sent folder, Troy would be wondering if he'd imagined the whole thing.

But there it was. And there she suddenly wasn't, suspiciously soon after he contacted her. So she'd rather get off the site entirely than reply, saying she wasn't interested? Cowardly. Contemptuous. If that was how she operated, Troy was lucky to have escaped.

His heart didn't seem to want to join in the outrage. Instead, it was acting as if he'd suffered a wrenching loss.

Would he ever stop being such an incurable romantic? Falling for women based on attraction and the fantasy promise of something really special, then staying consumed by them until the relationship blew up in his face? How long before he got a sensible Pavlovian response to women: pain, instead of fascination and arousal?

The chime of his email made him jump to check, cursing his eagerness. No, not from Foodie101. From Marie Hewitt. He opened the note, read it quickly. Then again more slowly while his brain struggled to catch all the implications.

Dear Troy,

I know this will seem a bizarre note. No, a really bizarre note. Maybe you know I already had a hand in setting up Justin and Candy, as well as our friend Kim and her fiancé, Nathan. My next project is to match up another member of Women in Power, Darcy Clark, owner of Gladiolas Restaurant. I just spoke with Darcy, and your name came up—I put two and two together and realized you'd met at Esmee last Wednesday.

This is way beyond the bounds of anything I should be doing in my professional capacity so take this communication as information shared between friends, and forget I'm the owner of Milwaukeedates.com.

Darcy is a wonderful woman, and will make the right man very happy someday. But she needs a little push in the romance direction in order to get past some fears. After speaking with her this evening, I'm convinced you're the man to do that pushing, and that she will eventually respond. It may take some patience in the meantime, but if you are really interested, I think you'll find she's worth the work it takes to win her.

Let me know if you want to talk further about this. Otherwise, put me down in the busybody column and hit Delete.

All the best,

Marie

Troy read the email a third time, adrenaline rising. Foodie101, his one-night lover, was Darcy Clark, the friend Candy and Kim talked about once in a while as strong, beautiful and talented, a woman who'd traded men for life in the kitchen. Even Justin had referred to her as a remarkable person, not particularly warmly, but then if she was a man-avoider, she probably hadn't fallen at his feet.

Darcy Clark. *Darcy.* He tried the name out a few more times.

All this time, Troy and his mystery woman had been connected through friends. Now that he thought about it, they'd missed meeting a few times already. If Darcy had been able to make Justin's sick-of-winter party back in February or if Troy had been able to make Kim's thirtieth birthday party in April, they would have met. If Justin had stayed even fifteen minutes longer at Esmee the other night, he would have recognized Darcy when she walked in.

How many other times had they circled so close? Would the intensity of their response to each other have been the same under different circumstances, and without the anonymity?

Darcy Clark. Adrenaline propelled him to his feet, sent him pacing. He knew who she was. He knew where to find her. He could see her again, relieve himself of the burden of wondering what might have been. Even though he could be putting his balls in jeopardy—as Steve, a fairly disgusting friend of Kim's brother, would have phrased it—Troy was going to take that chance.

Because he didn't think he'd be able to get the fantasy to stop torturing him any other way.

MARIE WALKED THROUGH ROOTS restaurant and down the stairs to the Cellar. Not her usual Friday-evening date with Quinn, but Darcy had called earlier and asked to meet her here tonight, her regular Monday off from the restaurant. Marie was relieved. It wasn't likely Darcy had arranged a public meeting at Marie's favorite haunt in order to scream at her again. Face-to-face they'd be able to work things out. Darcy would apologize for yelling last Saturday, then Marie would apologize for stepping over the line—except that in sending the email to Troy, she'd taken yet another step, and frankly, she wasn't averse to going further if necessary.

Maybe Quinn was right and she was overdoing the meddling, but instinct told her she was using justifiable means to reach a desirable and inevitable end.

She rounded the bottom step and saw Darcy right away,

looking radiant as usual in a low-cut white top under a teal sweater. She was laughing, leaning her dark head intimately toward an instantly familiar man, who was also laughing and leaning his dark head intimately toward her.

Quinn, halfway through a martini. Darcy, halfway through hers.

Marie's heart froze in her chest. They'd been there awhile? Together?

Quinn was speaking now, reaching to touch Darcy's forearm. She tipped her head to one side, listening raptly, her long, lovely throat exposed, her lush cleavage exposed.

Marie's heart: brutally exposed. How often had she told herself that Quinn and Darcy would make a perfect couple? And there they were, having found each other without her help, two strong, tall head-turners with striking personalities. Quinn was twelve years older, but relationships could go along nicely with that age difference, and Darcy was in many ways an old soul. She'd hinted here and there that her childhood and early adulthood were difficult, which could force a kid to mature early. Quinn was going to find someone sooner or later; he'd already admitted he was looking for something more serious than his usual array of casual flings.

Steady, Marie. Darcy wasn't Quinn's date for dinner and dancing this Friday.

Forcing herself to relax, she marched forward, determined to act as naturally as possible to prove to Quinn, and maybe to herself, that she could handle this. "Hello, there."

Quinn turned, ditto Darcy. Either they had nothing to feel guilty about or neither saw her as any type of threat, because they both broadcasted genuine welcome.

"I bumped into someone you know, Marie." Quinn gave his killer smile to Darcy, who beamed back. "It's great to meet one of your friends."

Marie would just bet.

"It's great that my friends are meeting each other." She congratulated herself for not sounding as if she were speaking through clenched teeth.

"Join us." Quinn indicated the seat on the other side of Darcy instead of the one next to him.

Not a problem. Everything was cool.

"Sit, Marie." Darcy got down from her stool. "I'm headed to the ladies' room. Back in a second."

Marie climbed onto the seat Quinn chose for her, determined to be cheerful and business-as-usual. "How are things? The situation at work resolved?"

He looked blank. Had Darcy erased his brain? She could undoubtedly do that to a lot of men. "The situation?"

"You said there was something you'd put a lot of effort into that wasn't working out."

"Ah." He rubbed his hand thoughtfully over his chin. "I remember now. Yeah, I think there still might be hope."

"Okay. Well. That's good." She hated that he seemed awkward talking about anything with her. That was a first.

And speaking of awkward firsts, they spent the next half minute in excruciating silence, shifting on their seats, glancing around.

To hell with business as usual, Marie would tackle him directly. "I guess you found out why I wanted to match you up with Darcy."

He nodded. "You were right. She is beautiful, and does seem strong and intelligent."

And thin and sexy and her legs went on for miles.

"Am I interrupting?" To her horror, she sounded like a bitter she-goat, and had to clear her throat. "Do you want me to come back later?"

"Yeah, Marie, that would be good." He nodded solemnly. "Because you're really cramping my style here."

Marie swallowed down panic, even suspecting he was joking. "I don't think you should go home with her."

"Ah, you don't." He signaled Joe the bartender, who'd made it over to their part of the crowd. "Marie, what'll you have?"

She had no brain to decide with. "What you're having."

"A martini for the lady tonight, Joe. And an order of chicken wings with the soy-tarragon sauce. Do you want anything to eat, Marie?"

She shook her head, stomach churning too hard for food. Too hard for alcohol, too, but she was going to need it.

"Just the wings, Joe." He turned to Marie, looking half amused, half annoyed. "So you don't think I should try to get Darcy into the sack."

Marie fidgeted, guiltily aware that it was none of her business whom he slept with, and that she had an ulterior motive for stopping him. "She's...well, I'm trying to set her up with Troy. I think there's something there. And if you— I don't know, maybe the two of you should try. But my gut tells me she really likes him."

"Hmm." He raised his martini contemplatively. Marie even thought the furrow between his eyebrows was sexy. She was hopeless. "There's a problem."

With giving up his chance at Darcy? "What's that?"

"You're cheating me out of a night of passion."

She couldn't stand it. Couldn't stand the idea of him writhing around in bed with her friend. Nameless bimbos Marie never had to see were bad enough. "You can't manage this one little disappointment?"

"No, this is serious business." Except he was looking less and less serious. His features were having a hard time staying in a frown, and his eyes were dancing. "I think a little compensation is in order."

"You— What do you mean?" Marie clutched the drink Joe set down in front of her.

"I mean you'll owe me for the lost night of ecstasy. I'll expect you to make it up to me."

Marie stopped breathing. The bar grew dim around her. All she could focus on was Quinn's handsome face, his eyes dark with amusement…and something else?

"I see." Her voice came out a hoarse croak. "Well, that sounds entirely…unreasonable."

"I'm joking, Marie."

"I know. I knew that." She forced a laugh, gulped her martini and barely got the swallow down, saving herself from repeated choking humiliation, thank God. Unfortunately, her most female parts hadn't caught up to the ha-ha-funny aspect of his trick and were still heated and hopeful. Would she never learn?

"However, I'm not above taking advantage and insisting you come to Chicago with me to have dinner and see a show. One of my favorite little theaters is doing a revival of *The Sound of Music*. I remember you saying you loved that musical."

Chicago. With Quinn. Another invitation, another whole evening in his company. This one would consist of a two-hour drive. Dinner. A show. Then the drive back in the intimacy of the wee hours. Or would they stay over somewhere? She couldn't let herself think that far. "I'd love it."

"Good." He pulled out his iPhone. "How about Saturday the twelfth?"

Marie pulled out hers, hands shaking so that she was barely able to manipulate the machine. "Um. Yes. I'm free. That sounds great."

"Good. I'll get us tickets and dinner reservations." He put his phone away, as calm and sane as she was rattled and neurotic. As if he did this every day with different women, and

Marie was simply up next. Except she didn't think he did this with other women. "I'm looking forward to it, Marie."

"Same here. Yes. Me, too. Thank you." She managed a smile; he smiled back easily. Oh, she wished she could get used to this.

"So you still think I was trying to get Darcy to sleep with me?"

"Weren't you?"

"Nope." He reached across Darcy's empty seat and touched her shoulder. "I'm in recovery from one-night-stands, remember?"

"Yes. But Darcy is…" Marie blinked and looked away from Quinn's mesmerizing gaze, trying to get her brain back on track. Something was nagging her subconscious, and she needed to stop and pay attention. What was it? Something about Darcy. And Troy. And Quinn? Matchmaking…Quinn wanting Darcy…Troy wanting Darcy…

Yes. There it was. Brilliant. She turned to Quinn, alight with excitement. "I have an idea."

"Oh, no." He let his head drop onto his hand, rubbed his forehead ruefully. "I know that look. The schemer is at it again."

"Will you help me?"

He groaned. "Can't you leave true love to run its natural, never-smooth course?"

"Its natural course would be for Darcy to run like hell from something that could be really good for her."

"And this is your responsibility why?"

"Because I care about her, and I want her to be happy. Weren't you going to match me up with someone for the same reason?"

"I was." He shook his head, eyes closed, but when he opened them again he was grinning. "I don't think there's another woman on earth I'd do this for, but okay, Marie. What part do I play in your soap opera?"

The only woman he'd do this for? Marie grinned back at him; he held her eyes and her smile, and for one beautiful second, she felt them connect on a level deeper than friendship, and felt the possibility, the real and wonderful possibility of her wildest dream coming true. Even with only that much of it fulfilled, she could cheerfully die from happiness right there.

But not until she filled Quinn in on her plan.

DARCY CAME BACK FROM THE bathroom, surprised to find Quinn at the bar alone. She glanced around; no sign of her friend. "Where's Marie?"

"She had an office crisis she had to take care of. Said if she didn't make it back tonight, she'd call you at home."

"Oh, okay." Darcy settled onto the stool next to him. She'd come here to apologize to Marie, but talking to Quinn was entertaining, and she still had half a drink to finish. If Marie would be calling later, Darcy could still make things right with her.

"So I guess it's just the two of us again." He lifted his martini toward her, expression warm. There was nothing overtly sexual about his behavior, but she sensed something in the atmosphere had shifted. A low buzz of excitement started in her chest. And ended abruptly when she thought of Troy.

Damn it. After one night nearly a week ago, he was not allowed to take over the rest of her life.

"I guess it is just the two of us." She clinked glasses, smiling into his eyes, which were stunning. Dark and deep and slightly turned down at the corners. He reminded her of someone. Some movie star. James Brolin? Young Alec Baldwin?

No, no, duh, George Clooney, how could she have missed it? Her crush of all silver-screen crushes. Same quirked eyebrows, bold chin, finely shaped head with neatly cropped graying hair. Yum. Everything about Quinn Peters fit the bill for a night of sweat and pleasure.

"What do you do for fun, Darcy?"

"Work is my fun. I run a restaurant."

He acknowledged her words with a quick nod. "Right. I knew that. Gladiolas. Very impressive."

"Have you been there?"

"Not yet." He turned his body toward her on the stool; his knee brushed the length of her thigh, making her skin come alive. The man was very, very sexy. And unless her receptors were on the blink, he felt the same way about her. So where did that leave Marie? Maybe Quinn thought they were just friends, but Darcy was pretty sure Marie had stronger feelings. Darcy might not be the world's most impressive moral role model, but she would never hit on a friend's love interest.

"I'll get you into Gladiolas some night and cook a private dinner." She arched an eyebrow. "For you and Marie…"

"That sounds interesting."

Not committing himself. Because he wasn't involved with or romantically interested in Marie or because he didn't want Darcy to know he was? "What do you do, Quinn?"

"I dabble."

"In?"

"Private investing."

"I see." She saw immediately that Quinn was probably loaded. And that his line of work would explain the jeans and casual blue shirt on a weekday afternoon. In a job like that he'd be very much his own boss, which made him even more attractive.

"So you never have any fun." He touched her arm. "Not even on special occasions?"

"Is this one?" She couldn't help smiling at him. He was irresistible.

"Meeting you could be nothing but a special occasion, Darcy."

"Re-e-ally." Oh, such a charmer. "And if I accept that compliment and return it, will I be causing any trouble for Marie?"

He didn't blink. "Marie and I are buddies."

"That's what she said, but I wasn't sure." She wasn't going to tell Quinn that she suspected Marie had, at very least, a killer crush on him.

"In fact, I'll tell you a secret." He beckoned her closer, touched his beautiful masculine lips to her ear, making it tingle with the desire for more touch. "She left just now so we could get to know each other better. Said she's been wanting to match us up for months now."

"Really." Darcy was astounded. Had she and the girls read Marie *that* wrong about this man? "You're sure?"

"She said as much." He signaled Joe. "Another drink, Darcy? While we get to know each other better?"

Darcy held his gaze. She was beginning to suspect what kind of getting to know each other he ultimately wanted to do. And why not? Maybe it was what she needed to erase the stubbornly lingering traces of Troy.

She sent him a smoldering look that was partly ruined when her conscience thumped on the inside of her skull. *Darcy, you moron, you don't want to do this.*

Yes, actually, she did. The guy looked like George Clooney. 'Nuff said.

"I'd love another drink." She drained the one she had, probably two ounces in a single shot, and rested the glass back on the bar, smiling determinedly. "Getting to know you better sounds like it could make my whole night."

6

DARCY DROVE SLOWLY UP E. Lake Forest Avenue, peering at the houses. Some numbers were visible, others not, but she was definitely close. Quinn's house would be in this block.

There. Number 819, an attractive brick Tudor with a bay window on the lower level, rounded front door, dormer on the second floor and a decent-size yard. Not the largest house on the block, not as ostentatious as she'd imagined, but in a neighborhood like this, not far from Lake Michigan, even a garage would be out of her price range.

She pulled opposite and parked, turned off the motor of her in-her-price-range red Kia Rio sedan.

Well. Here she was. This would all have been easier if she'd gone home with Quinn last night, the night they met. But he'd invited her for tonight, so what could she do? The problem was that the twenty-four-hour gap had taken away from the chemical momentum.

All day she'd been debating: to go or not to go? Quinn was undeniably attractive, and Darcy had talked to Marie last night to apologize and to hear from the horse's mouth that a "visit" between them would not be encroaching on her friend's man-territory or her heart's desire. Marie had been so enthusiastic about the idea of them getting together for a fling tonight that

Darcy had hung up feeling a little disoriented. Except Marie was so anxious to get Darcy into a relationship she'd probably tell Darcy to go ahead if the guy was a terrorist.

Tonight the guy was Quinn. And no matter how hard Darcy tried to focus her memory on his looks, his solid, mature body, his charm and appeal, she couldn't get more than a fuzzy image. Those martinis must have affected her more than she realized.

No matter. As soon as he opened the door and stood there in all his George Clooney glory, the rest of the night would fall into place.

She hoped.

Marie had also mentioned she'd be hosting a party at the end of the month for couples engaged and married over the last five years who'd met through Milwaukeedates.com, and was hoping to hold it at Gladiolas. Cutting it kind of close, but the restaurant didn't have many reservations that night, and if Marie chose food off of the regular menu, Darcy could manage it. No doubt Marie hoped Darcy and Quinn, or Darcy and Chaz or Darcy and *someone* would be there as a couple.

Not likely.

Her car door handle stuck; she used her shoulder to open it and stepped out into the darkening evening, which had turned chilly. The Kia's door contributed a loud thunk to the silent neighborhood when she closed it. Wild Tuesday night in Whitefish Bay, huh.

So.

Darcy stood staring at the house opposite. All she had to do was cross the street, walk up to the front door and ring the bell. So simple, even a child could do it. Why did it feel as if she needed a Ph.D. to manage? She should be excited, hot with anticipation for a night between the sheets with a sexy older man.

There was some of that, yes. But also an odd resistance. Nerves? Instinct?

Troy.

No. She crossed the street in exasperation, heels *chock-chocking* across the asphalt. She'd had her usual day off today, and had taken care with bathing and dressing, wearing a dark, flowery skirt with shades of red and blue and a clingy low-cut top in the same burnt-red color she'd painted her lips.

Troy was ancient history. A memory, even though it, yes, was a powerful one. It drove her crazy that she could barely remember Quinn's face, while Troy's features still haunted her with startling clarity. In weak moments she thought she should get his address from Justin, re-establish contact and see what this was about. In stronger moments she laughed at herself for even considering it. Reliably, like a Swiss watch, she was drawn to men who appointed themselves number one and couldn't be bothered to adjust their schedules or priorities or emotions for her sake. What made her think Troy would be any different? Just because she was hornier for him than any guy she'd met in a long time?

No. She was here, she was going to be with Quinn. They'd have a great evening, which would effectively erase any and all temptation to get herself involved with another guy who'd end up only appreciating that she cared for him because he cared so deeply for himself, too.

Up the front walk, the house loomed larger, almost spooky in its silence. Up the front steps, one, two, three, hand toward the doorbell and...

Darcy closed her eyes. She couldn't do this. Whether it was fear or solid instinct or what, resistance hit her like a meteor.

She turned and reached the first step toward retreat. The door swung open behind her.

Ugh! Busted. Quinn must have heard her. Fight or flight

kicked in. She wanted flight, to sprint back to her car and pull out in a screech of tires away from her terrible mistake coming here, back home to solitude and safety.

"Darcy."

She stiffened. Whirled around.

Troy. Tall and killer handsome in the warm glow from the front light. Her fight or flight instinct tripled, but this time she chose fight.

"What are *you* doing here?"

"I live here."

Darcy gaped. She'd gotten the wrong house? But she was sure the number matched what Quinn wrote down for her the night before at Roots. His handwriting had been clear and masculine, nothing scrawled or easy to mistake.

"I'm sorry. I was looking for—"

"Quinn." He stood solidly, feet planted slightly apart, hands on his hips, very much the immovable object. And an irresistible force, all in one dreamy, dark-eyed package.

Damn it. She was confused, horrified, pleased and hot for him, all at once, and it was confusing the heck out of her.

"*How* did you know I was looking for Quinn?"

"Sorry to say you've been punked, Darcy."

"Punked." She was still gaping, trying to figure out what the hell was happening while her brain was noticing all the sexy and oddly endearing things about him. Like the—

Wait, *Darcy?*

"How do you know my name is—" The obvious details clicked; she fisted her hands. "I am going to kill Marie."

"Marie, Quinn, me, we were all in on it. Triple homicide is a pretty bad deal." He gestured to the open door behind him. "Maybe you'd rather come in?"

"For what?" She was angry, tempted, repulsed, furious, excited, outraged, thrilled…and therefore going to be exhausted when all this was straightened out. At which point Marie would be lying lifeless, having just been fatally shrieked at.

Troy folded his arms across his beautiful chest and looked at her intently, which made her even more breathless and shaky than she already was. "Whatever would make you feel comfortable."

"What would make me feel comfortable is if you and Marie would stop manipulating me."

"I wanted to see you again."

"And you get your way no matter what? Even if it means sacrificing what I want?" What had she *just* been saying? Darcy muttered a few choice words about men and their pig-headed egos.

"You had no interest in seeing me again?"

"None."

"After that incredible night together."

"It was okay." She'd lost some of her safe outrage in the lie, and it showed in her tone.

"No urge to find out whether what's between us means anything more than animal attraction?" He started toward her.

She held her ground, fighting the urge to back down the stairs. "None."

"No urge to feel my hands on you, my mouth on you. My body over yours, under yours." His voice dropped to low, smooth temptation. "Inside yours."

"Zero." Her voice dropped, too, into the obvious emotional crackle of someone not telling the truth. She wrapped her arms around herself, hating her reaction to his approach.

"Zero." In less than a second, he took a last step, took hold of her upper arms and took possession of her mouth.

She slammed her hands to his chest, pushed him back. He lost balance and control for only half a second, stood solid again, watching her. Their breaths came out loud and harsh in the silent neighborhood.

Darcy should leave. Now. She should be forceful about putting an end to this farce while she still could. She should march out of here and teach him and Marie and Quinn a lesson about respecting her decision to stay away from this man—from any man.

Her feet wouldn't move. She couldn't tear her eyes away from Troy's.

Damn it.

She couldn't leave.

As if he read her mind, he moved in again, his lips soft and warm in the cool air, his taste and scent impossible to resist, drawing her to him until a wildfire of longing burned as powerfully as the first time, and Darcy lost herself to her body's sensual demands for this man's touch.

She let out a helpless moan, hating the sound, hating herself for needing this so much that she couldn't hold on to the defiant attitude that had seemed so important to her pride.

Troy broke the kiss; the silence was again filled with the sound of shallow, uneven breaths. She should say something. She should do something. She should collect her thoughts and act, be decisive and strong, and make sure he understood—

"It's still there." He spoke reverently, stroked her hair, touched her cheek, rubbed his thumb over her lips. "Whatever this is between us, it's still there. I didn't imagine it."

Darcy's only reaction was a convulsive swallow. She was overwhelmed, leaning against his chest, hers so full of emotion she couldn't speak.

"Come inside, Darcy—" he bent to kiss her again "—to tell me why, when you respond to me like this, you disappeared, why you ignored my email and took down your profile."

"I can tell you that now. Right here."

"Inside." He took three steps back, opened the door and gestured her in.

For a moment she rebelled. He'd gotten her here by trickery. He was insisting she come in. This was all feeling very manipulative and self-serving, and her alarm bells were ringing. No man would ever have her again who didn't care enough to compromise, who didn't care enough to give as well as receive, who expected her involved in his life, but made no effort to become involved in hers, made no effort to understand what was important to her.

Then she looked and saw that though Troy stood confident and calm, waiting, his eyes were anxious and vulnerable.

Aw, hell.

"Okay."

Air exited Troy's mouth and she realized he'd been holding his breath. Nearly comical, but somehow it wasn't in her to be disdainful of this man and his emotions, at least not right now, not tonight. Instead, she was touched.

Yeah, touched. In the head. Why was she leaving herself open to more disappointment? Letting down her guard meant passionate first feelings she might mistakenly think were love. It meant relaxing into coupledom, starting to believe that this time love could last forever. Then, inevitably, the courting period would be over, the demands begin for his every need to be met, along with the sudden indifference to hers.

All guys weren't like that. She knew that no matter how much she blustered and put on the big man-hater act, which burst out of her like anger. Not all guys, no.

Just the ones she fell for.

You could kick a dog only so many times before his loyalty wore out and self-protection and the survival instinct took over. Except the stupid hope wouldn't quit, the longing to get it right, the need to believe that *this* time maybe she'd learned. That *this* time maybe things could be different.

Marie thought she wasn't a romantic? She was too much of one.

She stepped into Troy's house, feeling as if she'd crossed a figurative threshold along with the literal one. The place was like him, relaxed, welcoming, but classy, in good taste.

A dog approached her, muscular and clean, reddish-gold with white around his muzzle and ears. Very pretty with intelligent eyes.

"This is Dylan. You like dogs?"

"Sure." She liked them when they didn't like her too much. The whole jumping, slobbering thing wasn't ideal, but Dylan seemed well-behaved, greeting her with a restrained sniffing bout and wagging tail.

She looked around while petting him, at good quality furniture, chairs and sofa upholstered in teal and beige with rust accents, and bright coordinating silk pillows. Looked at the television, but no recliner; at landscapes and prints on walls painted a pale orange; at lamps with multiple arms snaking out, tiny colorful shades on each bulb. At smooth stone sculptures on the mantel of the beautiful fireplace; at a tall, narrow vase filled with curly willow on an end table. In short, she looked everywhere but at him.

"Nice house."

"Mom's an interior decorator. The living room was my Christmas present, but I think it ended up more her present than mine. A little too decorated for my taste, but it's comfortable."

Darcy nodded, a fish out of water in Troy's elegant house. Even a mistake-glance at him brought back their skin-on-skin passion all night long at the hotel, and she wondered how she'd stay out of his bed this time and whether, if he made a move, she'd end up caring about anything but getting naked with him again.

"Would you like a drink?"

"I'd love it." More like needed it.

"Beer? Gin? Vodka? Tequila? Or I could open a bottle of wine."

"Wine would be nice. Red, if you have it." She was curious what he'd offer, moved around his living room, observing, touching, anything to hide her horrible awkwardness.

"Red wine coming up. Have a seat." He disappeared into the kitchen, which Darcy was dying to see, but refused to follow him, puppy style, especially since Dylan already had that job.

She blew out a breath and perched on the edge of the teal couch, pushing at magazines scattered on his coffee table: *Men's Health, National Geographic, Newsweek.*

So. They were going to have a talk. In Darcy's experience, talk was a euphemism for screaming first, lapsing into furious silence second.

She couldn't wait.

"Here you go." Troy brought two balloon glasses of red wine on a tray with a bowl of roasted almonds and offered them with easy grace. He was younger than she was by at least five years, but in this warm, stylish house she felt like an outclassed child.

He settled himself on the couch a cushion away, too close and not close enough. She could still catch his scent, was still yearning for the feel of his mouth. Happily, Dylan jumped up between them and settled, head on Troy's lap, tail thumping occasionally next to Darcy's thigh.

Darcy sipped her wine; no surprise, it was excellent.

"So, Darcy, you showed up here expecting to spend the night with Quinn." His voice was calm, matter-of-fact, but his face was tense, and his free hand rested on his lap in a fist.

Guilt. Darcy drank more wine, annoyed at her instant reaction. What did she have to feel guilty about? They'd signed no contract; hell, they hadn't even exchanged names. "That's right."

Troy abruptly got off the couch and paced the length of the room, no longer bothering to hide his agitation.

He was jealous. It hit her with a combination of horror, more guilt and a tiny thrill. She'd hurt him by agreeing to be with someone else. After only one night together.

That was crazy. If he'd wanted to do some other woman as beautiful and desirable as Quinn was handsome and desirable, thrash around in bed with her all night long, Darcy couldn't care less. She wouldn't blame him at all. You got happiness where you could.

For good measure she even made herself picture it. Troy all over some wildly hot female, like...Candy's model-gorgeous best friend, Abigail. Perfect.

The image stabbed like a knife slipped between her ribs. *Aw, hell.*

Troy stopped pacing, stood on the other side of the room, hands on his hips. "Why Quinn?"

"He was there. He was willing."

Troy snorted. "Unlike me."

"You..." Darcy closed her eyes, prayed for guidance, not to hurt him, but to get out of this intact. "You were too intense."

"Really." Troy moved back across the room toward her, speaking more quietly. "Too intense for what?"

"For me to keep seeing you."

"Because..."

"Because I'm not interested in starting a—"

"Relationship, so you said." He pushed impatiently at his hair, which fell back over his forehead. "The thing that interests me is that I went back over the night we had together, and I'm willing to bet everything I own that I said nothing about starting a relationship. I gave you no reason to think I was into anything but your incredible body and what it could do with mine. My email through Milwaukeedates only said I wanted to see you again. I don't think that's up there with asking for commitment on the first date."

Darcy could only stare, brain whirling. Why had she assumed? He'd said something that night, hadn't he? About her being his girlfriend? About the two of them long-term? Objected to her conditions of anonymity?

She couldn't come up with anything. But he had to have. Because otherwise…

"I'm thinking the idea of our starting a relationship had to have come from you." The silence in the room when he paused felt oppressive; she wanted to stand up and yell, or hurl her glass against his wall so it shattered. "Which means, Darcy, the fear came from your own feelings for me. For what we could have together."

She put her wine down, stood. "I should go."

"Ah." He grinned, but not with pleasure. "Too close to the mark?"

She took a few steps toward his front door. "I don't think—"

"Running away again, Darcy? Is that your answer to everything that touches you?"

She whirled on him. "You have no idea."

"Tell me and I will have an idea." His jaw set, his eyes were blazing; she had to hold herself back from sparking passion between them again. "Tell me everything and I'll understand completely. Until then I'm just thinking you're one closed off woman hiding a terrified little girl, not grown-up enough to give herself over to passion as intense as what we shared."

Darcy started to shake. She'd never felt this combination of fear and rage and desire so intensely in her life. She'd never felt anything as intensely in her life as what she felt around Troy. And yes, that made her want to run.

"I can tell you that I've had quite a few women in my life. Most of them were bad relationships, some were decent, but none started out with even half the power of what we shared. And I want to know what that is."

"It's called lust."

"Really." He was close now, standing in front of her, making her lift her chin to meet his eyes. "Lust, and that's it."

"Yes." Her voice gave her away again. "Male-female attraction, pheromones, electricity, whatever, but nothing—"

He launched a solid right-on-target attack on her lips that made her burn for him all the way down, then fight instinctively for her pride and her control and her sanity, setting herself against his hard chest, trying to budge the iron of his arms holding her at the same time she responded to his kisses with all the passion she couldn't seem to control around him.

Troy didn't give, didn't acknowledge her weak struggle, but pushed until her back hit the wall and he pressed his body against her, the hard bulge in his jeans finding her softness unerringly, making her burn hotter still.

She clutched his shoulders, aroused out of her mind not only by the contact, but the male force of his determination to have her, to claim her. The rhythmic push between her legs told her in no uncertain terms what he wanted from her, and within ten seconds, she wanted it as much as he did.

Damn him. Damn this power he had, damn the way she responded to the sleek muscle under her fingers, to the male scent of him, to the way his hands explored her, demanding, possessive, so sure of the territory of her body, her most private possession.

How could the pleasure be this strong when only agony would follow?

Her top and bra were yanked up; her breasts spilled free into the cool room, covered immediately by his warm mouth, sucking and pulling one nipple, the other rolled between his fingers, stroked by his palm.

She moaned, her head bumping against the wall. His other hand snaked up her skirt, dipped into her panties; his fingers brushed the clipped hair between her legs, then slid deeper, seeking and finding her moisture.

"Troy." Everything she wanted from him was contained in that syllable. He teased her, tantalized her with his fingers and hot mouth until her legs nearly gave way and she had to push back hard to stay upright.

He went to his knees at her feet, pushed up her skirt, hauled down her panties and buried his mouth between her legs, sending slippery warmth over her clitoris, jamming her spine against the wall.

Darcy cried out at the sensation, at the bold strokes of his tongue. His finger joined, slipping inside, pushing rhythmically, finding a place deep inside her that nearly made her scream from pleasure. Her hair fell over her face, her body broke out in a sweat. Her head banged back, but there was no pain. Nothing except this man and his tongue and hands on her.

She heard herself moan and pant, her hands scrabbled to clutch something, to brace herself. She found nothing, reached helplessly up the wall, legs opening higher, giving him more and deeper access until her climax started an inevitable climb, a powerful wave that came from a distance, gathered everything in her and burst into a blinding finale.

Over and over she pulsed, losing her ability to stand, sliding down the wall to collapse in a sweating, panting heap on the floor of his living room.

He was out of his pants already, his erection proud and rigid, straining toward her as if he had a homing device, and she was home.

The sight was beautiful, rekindling her arousal. She got to

her knees, took him in her fist, keeping her eyes fixed on his erection, too vulnerable to meet his gaze after the way she'd exploded against his mouth. She worked her hand in a steady, gentle rhythm, while the fingers of her other hand explored and manipulated the soft sacs of his testicles.

Thirty seconds he stood it, then moisture spread from the tip of his cock. He reached down for his jeans, yanked a condom out of the pocket and rolled it on.

If he made love to her face-to-face, she'd be lost. Her softie heart would weaken; she'd start thinking she was falling for him. Everything would go to hell from there.

She got to her knees on his carpet, fell forward onto her hands and lifted her skirt so her bare ass faced him and there would be no question what she was offering.

He groaned, knelt behind her and steadied her, pressed the head of his penis against her opening, a push that relented only to push farther, deeper inside her. She was plenty wet; another push slid him in all the way, making her moan and arch her back with pleasure.

For one blissful second, he held still, hands firm on her hips, cock filling her. Then when she thought she'd go mad unless he moved, he began to ride her, slowly, then faster, slapping against her, his fierce rhythm echoed by his harsh breathing. Instinct told Darcy he wouldn't last long, and she felt a thrill of feminine power. She was not the only one flattened by this wild emotion passing between them.

Another minute, maybe less, and his breath stopped, his rhythm faltered, then sped, stopped altogether and he pushed hard, then again, contracting into her.

Darcy closed her eyes, overwhelmed by his ecstasy, almost more than she had been by hers.

Was this destined to evolve into love?

No, no. With love always came pain. And fear. And disappointment.

Troy wrapped his arms around her and brought her up to her knees, her back to his chest, kissing her neck, her cheek, her hair. She turned her face and their lips met in a kiss so tender her eyes threatened to fill with tears.

And once again, from the depth of her wounded, beaten and still-naive soul came hope that somehow with this man she'd find the love she'd craved her entire life.

7

TROY CAME BACK INTO THE LIVING room, having disposed of the condom, to find Darcy dressed and looking ready to leave.

No. She was not leaving. Not after this miracle of finding her again.

"Got what you came for?"

Her face fell. "I should go."

He came to a stop a few feet away, jammed his hands on his hips to keep from reaching for her. Touching her was like a drug he craved. She fit his hands. Her breasts, her gorgeous ass, her firm belly, all of her enticed him, called to him. Around her he was completely depraved. "Why?"

"Because..." Her expression became slightly panicked.

"Because if you stay, you might enjoy yourself? And that would be horrible, to have a good time with me, because then you might want to see me again and that would be the worst thing that happened since the black plague?"

She laughed in surprise; he had to cement his hands harder. When she laughed the tension fled from her face and body and she came irresistibly alive. "Maybe not that bad."

Dylan approached, wagging his tail, sniffing curiously at Darcy's knees. Troy had a brainstorm.

"Tell you what. I have to walk Dylan. Come with me. Fifteen minutes, half an hour tops. I think even you can handle that level of commitment."

Her smile faded, but she didn't look as defensive. "I guess I can."

Good dog, Dylan. He made sure his face didn't show triumph. "Let's go."

They took Troy's usual route, out onto his street, toward the lake, then north for a short time on Lake Drive, which wound along Lake Michigan's shore, dotted with some of the city's most spectacular homes, then another left. If everything went well, he planned to extend the walk considerably, maybe tempt her successfully into spending the night.

"Nice to live near the lake."

"It is." He'd taken the lead from her, providing small talk, hoping to be able to sense the moment when he could take the conversation in a more personal direction. There wasn't much he didn't want to know about her, but he knew enough already to understand that if he pushed too hard, Darcy would clam up like a…clam. "Did you grow up in the city?"

"Waukesha. We lived on both floors of a duplex."

"We…"

"Mom, Dad, my younger sister and me."

"They still around here?" He paused to let Dylan sniff a particularly inviting spot off the sidewalk, and to add his territory mark if it turned out to be necessary from a dog perspective.

"They are." She spoke grimly. "Brit lives in Glendale. Married with kids. My parents are still in Waukesha. Not married."

"I'm sorry."

"Don't be. They split the day after Brit graduated high school. They should have done it years sooner."

"Not happy together." Stating the obvious, but he wanted her to keep talking.

"Not happy. Dad's an alcoholic, Mom's an enabler. He'd throw fits, she'd respond with passive aggressive crap until she finally blew and threw something at him."

"Great relationship role model for little girls."

"I'm sure it's why I've done so well." She snorted. Their fingers bumped. He stuffed his into his pocket to avoid taking her hand.

"We look for what we know."

"I know not to look." She sent him a glance he couldn't decipher. "What about your family?"

"We lived one of those perfect-family lives that wasn't so perfect. Dad was not a drinker, but he was something of a dictator. I spent a lot of time trying to protect my mother and younger brother, which wasn't my place."

"I did that, too." Something in her tone made him turn to look at her. She was watching him almost eagerly, and he had to battle again the need to touch her, kiss her, make her his for the rest of time. The least successful way to keep a woman like Darcy was to try to. "I also felt it was my duty to protect my mother and my sister from Dad's temper and his irrational need to control. It doesn't work."

"No. It doesn't." They continued walking, Dylan's leash jingling in the darkness. "I guess that means you clashed most often with your father."

"You might say that." She spoke dryly but he felt he knew intimately the pain behind her words.

"That was my job, too. He came down hardest on my younger brother, put the most pressure on him. Tom paid him back by becoming an unemployed addict."

"Oh, I'm sorry. Are you in touch with him?"

"Occasionally. He's hard to reach." Troy sighed. "Literally and figuratively."

She nodded beside him, a simple gesture, but he felt she understood. "And your mom?"

"She stuck with him. Her capacity for denial is infinite."

"I thought my mom's was, too. But when Dad was fired for drinking and she had to get a job, suddenly she realized she wasn't helpless. And then he realized the same thing, so he came down on her even harder. How dare she not need him? How dare she enjoy her life?" She laughed bitterly, shaking her head. "Well, it's done now. They got rid of us, got rid of each other, but kept the hatred and anger, which is so gosh darn healthy."

"This have anything to do with your reluctance about relationships?"

"Maybe. I don't know how you get rid of wiring that deep."

"I don't, either." To put it mildly. Troy was always falling for manipulative women, Debby being the latest and most consummate damsel in distress. Everything that happened to her was an emergency. Everything that didn't happen to her didn't register. And there he'd been, Sucker in Shining Armor, trying over and over to rescue and protect her from the big bad world. Only after she'd used him up did he really understand that she didn't want to be rescued. Without her distress Debby would become merely another damsel—her biggest fear.

"Are your parents still together?" Darcy asked.

"Yes. Still living the perfect country club life in River Hills, where I grew up."

"And here you are slumming in Whitefish Bay."

"Guilty as charged." He sent her a rueful smile. "I did make it to L.A. for college, so I haven't been an East Sider all my life. Only a mere eighty-five percent."

"Tiny fraction." She turned toward the lake while they let Dylan sniff again; the breeze blew back her hair; her face was pale and serene in the light from the streetlamps. She looked like an ivory statue of a goddess.

This time Troy responded to his instinct, turned her toward him, pressed his lips to her temple, then reached lower and found her surprised mouth, cool from the night air.

She exhaled when he drew back. "What was that for?"

"The hell of it." He took her face in his hands and kissed her again, as lingeringly as he dared. "And because you are too beautiful not to touch. It would be a complete waste of my time keeping my hands to myself."

She made a scornful noise, but had to hide a smile. He released her and kept walking, following Dylan's insistent tug, trying to hide how deeply her kisses rattled him. Nearly as much as her recent openness, so different from the last time they were together, when she wouldn't even tell him her name. Troy was daring to hope, a dangerous pastime. He was in this too deep already. Hell, he'd been in too deep the second they made eye contact at Esmee Restaurant.

Silence stretched; they turned left on the next street. Troy waited, full of questions, but hoping she'd start asking this time so she wouldn't feel under interrogation.

Twenty seconds later, his patience was rewarded. "Who turned you onto arak?"

"My friend Chad. His mother is Lebanese. He also recommended Esmee."

"Where do you know him from?"

"High school friend. Got me the job at SoftCare, Inc., where he works in sales. We also compete in triathlons together a few times a year."

"Ah." She flashed him a flirty grin, visible under a streetlight. "That explains the flawless bod."

"Thanks." He barely managed to hide the charge he got out of her compliment. "What explains yours?"

"Ha!" She laughed. "Not even close. But thank you."

"You're no judge." He nudged her with his shoulder; their fingers bumped again. He did take her hand that time, for a few steps, then squeezed and released before she could balk and pull away herself. She moved off for a few steps, then came back, which made him absurdly happy.

"What is SoftCare about?"

"We provide care management software to client companies that have to keep track of patients."

"Which means..."

"Which means really sick people can have all their information in one place and a nurse care manager coordinates all the medical care, works with the families, et cetera."

"You do what there?"

"I'm the IT director. I manage the technical stuff in-house to make sure the company runs smoothly. I help the sales force make recommendations to potential clients."

"And you wrote a book."

"Justin wrote the book. I did the geek stuff, the online interactive part. People read the chapter either in book form or online, then work with the hands-on demos to learn how to maintain and get full use from their PCs, troubleshoot when things go wrong and so on."

"Sounds brilliant." She bent to pet Dylan, who'd crossed to sniff something near her feet. "If the book takes off, will you quit your job?"

"Only if I have something satisfying to do instead. Volunteer work, maybe. I'd love to teach basketball, maybe mentor kids, get them turned onto fitness in some form. Maybe get certified to counsel drug and alcohol addicts. Probably in some sense an attempt to make up for not being able to help my brother, Tom."

She looked up, her face soft with sympathy. "That's an honorable goal."

Troy shrugged, trying to hide his pleasure at Darcy's admiration, and trying not to feel envious of Dylan with her hands all over him. That had to be a new low, wishing he was a dog. "Tell me about Gladiolas."

"Most of the time it's hell. But it's my hell, and I signed on for it, so I suppose I love it."

"You suppose...?"

"I do." She sighed, straightening to continue their pace. "It's everything I've wanted and worked for. It got me sober, gave me something to live for. The hard part is realizing most restaurants don't survive, and trying not to look at this as my only shot."

He nodded. Similar to how he felt about her, even though it was ridiculously soon after he met her to be having those worries. "But Gladiolas is doing really well."

"So far. But...stuff happens."

He glanced at her. Her mouth had set into a tight line again. His instinct prodded him. There was more there. "Like what, for instance?"

"Like some jerk you fired gets back at you by opening a nearly identical restaurant in the same town."

"Oh, nice." The pain in her voice made him want to find whoever this guy was and punch him out. "Is this a done deal?"

"He's opening at end of the month. Got a wealthy investor, ideal location."

"Sorry to hear that."

"Thanks." She pushed her hair back with both hands, then let it fall. He felt she needed more from him, but he had nothing to give. He'd learned with Debby that if he tried to solve a partner's problems, he only ended up responsible for issues that weren't his to fix, and she ended up incapable of acting on her own behalf.

"Tell me how you got into cooking."

"Mom was a terrible cook, so I did most of the food in

our house. I always loved it. Seemed natural to get a job in a kitchen as soon as I could work. The chef took me under his wing, got me to stop self-destructive behavior and sent me on the straight and narrow."

"Drinking."

She nodded. "Chip off the old block. I was able to stop the abuse without giving it up. My sister Brit is in recovery, has been for nearly a decade."

"Good for her." He slowed their pace. She wasn't only talking, she was pouring out her life. The contrast with the other night was stark. Did she just need anyone to listen, or had she decided to trust him? He didn't think she'd tell him all this if she was never planning to see him again. The thought made him want to jump around like a kid.

"As Darcy's World Turns." She gave a harsh laugh. "I have no idea why I'm dumping all this on you."

"Because I asked? Because I wanted to know?"

"Hmm, guess that might be it, yeah."

They turned left on Danbury, Troy plotting how to get her back inside his house when they reached his street.

"So, chef, tell me your fantasy meal."

"My fantasy meal?" Darcy cocked her head, thinking; her hair swung to the right, exposing her smooth neck, giving Troy another reason to get her inside. Everything she did turned him on. "You won't believe me."

"Sure, I will. What is it, truffled foie gras with lobster champagne sauce and caviar?"

"Nope. A giant bag of potato chips and a Diet Coke, eaten at the beach."

"Seriously?" He turned to gape. "You're a potato chip freak?"

"Freak wannabe. I rarely buy them because if they're around I won't stop eating them."

"And so...on this beach after your bag is finished, what's for dessert? Chocolate in some form?"

"More chips."

"Wow. You've got it bad." He grinned, wanting to take her hand again. He loved that this sophisticated chef could get into junk food. "Wavy or regular?"

"Regular. No flavor, just plain with salt. God, I love them. If I get to heaven, that's my reward. Bags and bags with none of the caloric implications."

Troy nodded, thinking of the unopened family-size Lay's Classic potato chips sitting in his cabinet. He might have an in there.

"What's your perfect meal?"

"Mine?" Troy frowned, reeling Dylan in from a too-deep foray into someone's yard. "I would have felt a little weird talking about this to a chef, but after hearing yours is potato chips... Mine is a pretty basic guy meal. A grilled burger, medium rare, on a sesame roll, with a slice of tomato, sweet onion, lettuce, pickle, catsup and mustard."

"Nothing wrong with that. What else?"

"French fries. Hot and crisp."

"Shoestring or steak fries?"

"Shoestring." He tugged Dylan along. "Coleslaw, not too mayonnaisy, not too sweet. And cold beer to wash it down."

"Dessert?"

"Chocolate milkshake."

"You *are* a guy."

"Told you. The most important thing is that the meal has to be eaten after a workout. Sexual or otherwise."

She giggled. "Why then?"

"Everything tastes better when your body is tired from being pushed to the limit."

"Hmm." She turned and gave him a provocative once-over. "I kind of like the idea of your body pushed to the limit."

"Yeah?" He took her hand again, determined to keep it this time.

"Maybe I should install an exercise room at Gladiolas."

"You should. For before and after the meal. Keep people coming back."

"I'll keep that in mind." She'd fallen into step beside him, gently swinging their clasped hands. Not pulling away. He felt like he'd struck gold.

They turned back onto E. Lake Forest, ambled the rest of the way back to his house. He'd considered stretching the walk out longer, but the air was cooling rapidly, and he had high hopes since the tension had relaxed between them that she'd stay. Awhile at least. Overnight maybe. He was still starved for her, wanted her again, in his bed this time, and all night.

Up his front walk, she fell silent and he felt her tension growing again. "You hungry? Want something to eat? I'm not sure my ego can handle providing food to a chef, but I can probably find something you'd like."

"I'm… I was thinking I should go."

"Yeah?" He unlocked his door, unclipped Dylan's leash and held the storm door open so she could follow the dog inside. She hesitated only a second before she went in. He kept the smug expression off his face, stepped inside and gave in to an impulse by double-locking the door behind him. "Go where?"

"Home. Did you just lock me in?"

He grinned at her, tossed his keys on the table next to the door. "You are my prisoner until I decide to let you leave."

"I see." Her brow furrowed, but her eyes sparked excitement that gave him hope. "So I have no say in this whatsoever?"

"None."

She folded her arms across her chest. He all but held his breath.

"It's only fair to let me know what your evil plans are."

Troy made his smile as evil as he could given that triumphant joy was his emotion of the moment. "I'm going to feed you potato chips until you beg for mercy."

"Um." Darcy frowned in mock confusion. "That's supposed to be a threat?"

"Then—" he advanced menacingly, keeping his voice a low, dark drawl "—I'm going to carry you upstairs and make love to you until you're unable to walk."

"I'm sorry." She shook her head in bewilderment. "I'm not understanding. *When* does the evil part kick in?"

He swooped forward, caught her lips with his. She responded, clutching his shoulders, pressing her body close.

"I may be a lame villain, but I can tell you if you keep pushing against me like that, you don't get the potato chips until later."

"Ooh." Her voice was low and throaty. "That *is* evil."

"Come." He took her hand and started for the stairs before she could change her mind.

"Wait, no. Excuse me." She pulled her hand away; his heart skipped. "I believe the deal was that you would carry me."

He groaned in mock dismay, then lunged and picked her up in an undignified fireman's carry, her head dangling down his back. "Okay, okay."

"This…is not…what I had in…mind." She giggled through her protest; he'd never heard a sweeter sound.

"No?" He pretended to stagger on the stairs, making her squeal. One of her shoes clattered to the floor.

"No! I was thinking Rhett Butler in *Gone with the Wind*."

"Rhett who? Gone with the what? Is that some chick flick?" He reached the top of the stairs, turned toward his room, kicked open the door and laid her on his bed with just enough force to make it feel as if he'd dumped her there à la Rhett.

She struggled to sit up, but he was there first, covering her body with his, finding her mouth, tasting it in the darkness of his room. Her giggles stopped abruptly; she opened to him, legs tangling with his. Her other shoe dropped off the bed. Even the thought of her bare feet excited him.

He lifted off her, determined this time that passion wouldn't carry them away, that they'd be able to take it slow, make their lovemaking last. Her skirt came down leisurely; its elastic waistband saved him tackling complicated fastenings. His eyes had adjusted enough to see her legs as soft cream against his hunter-green bedspread, which looked black in the dim light spilling in from the hallway. He eased down her panties, brushing his hand across the dark hair between her legs.

Her heaven might be full of potato chips. His was full of Darcy.

She lifted to sitting and took off her shirt while he did the same, then he sat transfixed while she unhooked her bra, hesitating for a delicious moment before she let it slide off, making him groan with pleasure.

"Your breasts are so beautiful," he whispered. Her nipples called to him, dark small circles on the pale perfection of her skin. He took one into his mouth, loving her quick intake of breath, fumbling to lower his jeans, reluctantly breaking his hold to kick those and his underwear off the bed so he could return to worship, sucking her neglected other nipple, fondling the still-moist first one with eager fingers.

"You are so beautiful, Darcy. So sexy." He felt her stiffen, told himself to hold back, not overwhelm her, saying phrases she'd probably heard many times from other men. Like the woman in the Arabian Nights story, instinct told him he had to offer something she hadn't had before if he wanted a chance to get into her heart. "You drive me wild. I'm like a raging… rhinoceros."

Her stiffness relaxed. "Say what?"

"While *you,* you are my sensual, stunning rhinoceros-ess."

She giggled. "I'm pretty sure I've never been called that before."

"So you see…I'm not like other men you've known."

She laughed, pushing suddenly, her strong arms catching him off balance, tumbling him to the mattress. She followed, took over, exploring him with her mouth, soft hair dragging across his chest, adding to the sensation. Her hands followed, raking his skin lightly. Her tongue found his nipple, swirled around, it teeth gently biting. He moaned as she moved downward; his penis stiffened in anticipation.

Her mouth closed over him, took him in deep, making air rush from his lungs. "Darcy."

"Mmm?"

"That is…oh, man."

She backed off to slide her lips firmly up and down the sensitive underside of his cock, fisting him sometimes, using her fingers to manipulate his balls. He was overwhelmed with the sensations, yes, turned on out of his mind, but also with a piercing tenderness, a humbling opening to her that she'd no doubt scorn if she knew he was feeling it so deeply and so soon.

What was he going to do with his passion for this woman?

He took her shoulders, lifted her up, intending to turn her onto her back. But she resisted, positioned herself on top, straddling him, her hips moving forward and back, up and down the length of his erection so the soft lips of her sex stroked him, clung and rubbed, leaving their moisture behind. Her hair hung in a curtain over her face; her breasts swung heavy and free. She was aroused, too, her lips parted, eyes half-closed, face tense with concentration.

He nearly shamed himself by coming onto his belly.

"Condom?"

Troy pointed to the drawer of his nightstand, unable to speak. She reached, found one, ripped the package and rolled it over him, using lingering movements of her hand to make even that a sensual experience.

Darcy Clark was a miracle. One he wanted to experience over and over.

She leaned forward, lifted, took his straining cock in her hand and moved it back and forth again over her sex, this time catching her clitoris on the upslide, pulling it on the down, circling the bud with the tip of his penis, then stroking again. She gave a soft cry, breath coming faster; her movements lost their easy rhythm.

He wanted to be inside her more than he wanted to go on living. Every time his cock dipped toward her entrance, a surge of desire made him want to grab her and push in. But he wanted this to be good for her, more than for him.

So he watched, waited, clenching his teeth, fighting the lust. Once more she arched, pulled his penis to her clitoris, circled her hips, eyes closed, the most beautiful thing he'd ever seen. Down again, then suddenly with a quick glide she settled and he disappeared up inside her.

Her walls clutched him tightly; he nearly yelled with his impatience, took hold of her hips and pushed her up, down, forcing himself up hard inside her, over and over, selfish now, past all reason.

She let out a taut breath, then took up his rhythm, rode him sitting astride, her pleasure reflected in her face. He watched her, trying desperately to hold back from coming. His thumb found her clitoris, he rubbed her, crazy emotion washing over him as he saw her starting to come apart, her poise and concentration broken, desperation tinging her movements.

A light sweat broke out on her body. Her breathing became erratic. She was close. He let himself build toward his own climax, controlling it with every ounce of willpower left to him so he could get there with her.

She said his name in a low, urgent voice, said it again. He

reacted with tenderness so fierce it made him grit his teeth in pain. Too soon to turn what was inside him into speech. He'd have to tell her with his body.

Maybe Darcy heard him, because she arched into bliss, gasping again and again, as her walls contracted around him, and Troy finally let go, thrusting up once, twice, three times and his own orgasm tore through him while the words played in his head. *Darcy. I love you.*

He'd never been so sure of anything and never been filled with more fear or dread over an emotion so often celebrated with joy. He loved her. *Help.*

"Mmm." Darcy collapsed onto his chest and lay there, her body heavy and sweet with satiation. "Wow."

He wrapped his arms around her, stroked her hair, wanting to protect her, love her and imprison her all at the same time, still unable to speak. Yes. Wow.

She lifted her head, rained tiny kisses over his chest and slowly pulled off him. He winced at the loss of connection, accepted the very practical tissues she handed him, and got rid of the latex in a three-point toss across the room.

"Troy."

Something about her tone made him instantly wary. He forced his body to stay relaxed, resisted the urge to pull her to him, make her lie down against him and stay there all night. Once again he was horribly raw and open to a woman who could hurt him viciously just by walking out the door. "Yeah?"

"I have something to tell you."

"Sure." He was glad she wasn't lying against him because his attempts to relax had just gone out the window and she'd feel the rigidity of his muscles. Here came the lecture, the I-don't-want-to-get-involved lecture, the this-was-just-sex lecture. "What is it?"

"You took care of my sexual needs tonight and it was really great. And I really appreciate it."

"Okay." He clenched his jaw, pain hovering at the ready. Here it came.

"But now…" She gestured toward his door.

"Right." He felt a deep burning disappointment in his chest. "Now you need to leave."

"No." She giggled and leaned forward to kiss his cheek. "Now I need those potato chips."

8

"SO TELL ME."

Darcy pushed closer into Troy's embrace. She couldn't believe how peacefully she'd slept, couldn't believe how peaceful she'd felt waking up to him. Usually she came to with a jolt, ready to attack the day's challenges. This morning she'd felt as if her brain had to push through molasses to surface.

He'd already been awake when she opened her eyes, must have been studying her while she slept. His expression was tender and sweet—until she'd yawned and stretched, pressing her nakedness against his side, and then he'd been ready to go again, bless his young male heart.

Now, after extended languorous lovemaking, she was a boneless jellyfish of a woman. "Tell you what?"

"Tell me what you have against men."

Darcy's lovely relaxation fled. "Oh, there's a nice one. 'Good morning, Darcy, how about sex followed by a nice stroll through a minefield?'"

"I'm going to want to see a lot of you, Darcy."

"Do I have a say in this?"

"Not really, no."

She ignored the thrill and snorted derisively. "Well, there's a good start to answer your question about what I have against men."

"Hmm. I'm guessing your boyfriends didn't give you much say in anything."

"They let me dress myself."

"Oh, hey!" His eyes lit up. "I can allow that, too!"

"Oh, you're a prince. All that freedom? I wouldn't know what to do with myself."

He squeezed her to him, nuzzling her hair. "I'm not out to control you, change you or enslave you, Darcy. I'm asking for the chance to be with you, to find out what this is. If it's just lust and burns itself out, fine, nothing wrong with a good old-fashioned sexual marathon."

She giggled, relieved the discussion had stayed light. "Hey, you could add that to your events. Running, biking, swimming and sex. A quadrathlon."

He laughed; she loved that he got her humor. She was stupidly loving everything about their time together. Shouldn't warning bells be going off like mad? They were frustratingly silent. How was she supposed to panic properly at a time like this?

She needed to remind herself that relationships—yes, okay, okay, this was starting to look like one—were always beautiful at the beginning. Even her parents must have been utterly enthralled with everything about each other at one time. Impossible to imagine given the deep discontent bordering on hatred that comprised most of their interaction through her childhood.

"Men…?"

Darcy sighed and curled his arm tighter around her. "Men. Right."

"They haven't treated you well."

"I haven't chosen well. I finally decided since I was doomed to repeat the same punishment in my relationships, I'd be happier and healthier avoiding them."

"So what happens if you find a man who is nice to you?" She blinked sweetly at him. "Got anyone in mind?"

"No, no, no. A completely random question."

She rolled onto her back and stared at the ceiling, her left side still flush against his. She had some kind of weird addiction to the feel of his skin. And muscle. God, he was all muscle. She'd love to watch him work out sometime, revel in his strength and the contract-extend ripple under his skin as he—

Wait, what were they talking about?

Oh, right, men. "Here's the thing. My parents were madly in love when they got married. I have divorced friends who were madly in love when they got married. If I'd married any of the men I was madly in love with, it would have been a complete disaster. I don't trust the feeling."

He was quiet so long she tilted her head to see his face, above hers on his down pillows. He was gazing across the room, but bent to brush her lips with his when she turned, started stroking her stomach absently. Oh, she loved the way he touched her, as if it was instinct, something he didn't even have to think about. The man probably gave back rubs in his sleep.

"Darcy, I'm not sure how to put this, and thanks for the proposal, but I'm not quite ready to discuss marriage with you."

She started spluttering in shock until she saw his lips curve and realized he'd gotten her. She shoved playfully at his side. "Okay, okay. Your point is that it's not going to kill me to keep seeing you and having incredible sex."

"That's exactly my point. And maybe to keep your mind open to the idea that not all men are out to enslave you." He frowned. "Though the concept has its attractions. You naked and chained to my bed, for example. I could get into that. Maybe giving me a massage every night. A home-cooked meal twice a day. Laundry, doing my errands, washing my feet and—"

Darcy launched herself at him, and discovered to her delight that this tall, buff man was horribly ticklish. And way too strong. She found herself pinned back on the bed within seconds, totally helpless. Terrible flashback to the one time Chris had gotten physical in his anger—anger over being caught cheating and anger over her gall to be upset about it. *"Let go."*

He did immediately, searching her face. "Hey, you okay?"

"Yes, sorry, sorry." She gave a nervous laugh. "I attacked, you defended. You were playing. It was fine. I overreacted."

He kissed her mouth, a long, sweet kiss so gentle that she could feel her lips trembling. How did he manage to make his way past so many defenses before she even knew she was under siege? "Darcy, I have never used, nor will I ever use strength to dominate, control or hurt anyone. Anyone. Especially you."

Her heart started performing feats out of *Alice in Wonderland,* swelling to enormous proportions, then shrink-melting into a goopy warmth spreading through in her chest. "I believe you."

"Thank you." He smiled then, a direct, relieved beautiful smile that crinkled the corners of his eyes under his morning-rumpled hair and turned him entirely irresistible, this young man who made her feel so damn much. "Tell me more."

She rolled her eyes, shaky still. "Always the questions. Boyfriend one in college, Jon, insisted I put his agenda, friends and desires ahead of mine."

"Is there something wrong with that?"

Darcy laughed at his fake-shocked expression. "Boyfriend two after college, Chris, couldn't handle my hours and devotion to my career and cheated on me with a woman who loved nothing better than to wash his socks."

"Wait, you don't love washing socks?" He frowned, clearly struggling. "I'm having serious doubts about your suitability as a woman."

"Exactly."

He grinned and turned her away from him, started stroking her back, kneading muscles that were less tense than usual, but no less grateful for his attention. "How about nonboyfriend men? You don't have good male friends? Brothers?"

"No brothers. I hung around with guy friends in college and in restaurant kitchens, but all my close friendships have been with women." She stirred uncomfortably. Most of her male friends had been drinking buddies or colleagues. As for her female friendships, she wasn't the type to keep people posted on all her feelings the way some women could. Her sister, Brit, could talk emotions all day, probably because of her therapy and A.A. meetings. Amy at the restaurant had no problem sharing. Candy certainly could. Marie and Kim were more guarded. But then most people were more guarded than Candy, bless her.

So Darcy wasn't likely to win any intimacy awards.

"What about the chef who encouraged you?"

"God, yes, without him I'd probably be an abused-wife drunk." She shuddered at the thought, then turned in Troy's arms. "Enough of me. I want to hear your stories. Unless you've always had perfect relationships, then keep it to yourself."

His eyes were warm. "If I'd had perfect relationships I wouldn't be here with you."

"Good point." She touched his cheek, rough with stubble. "I'm glad they sucked."

He grinned. "This is the first time I've ever said this, but so am I."

"Tell me." She traced the fine arch of his eyebrows, drew her finger gently down the noble line of his nose to his lips, which opened and gently closed around her first knuckle.

"There's not much to say. I've had unhealthy patterns, too. Never got it right."

"So we're relationship misfits."

"Looks that way."

She contemplated the masculine beauty of his face, absently thinking someone should do a sculpture of him. "So why don't we be together as much as we want and not call it a relationship, so we can't screw it up."

He laughed. "You know, I think that might work."

"Good." She grinned and launched herself on top of him, snuggling down on his broad chest, feeling his arms come tightly around her, acknowledging, yes, that just maybe Marie was a little bit right, and this was what she wanted.

"Just don't forget that because of a man you're a brilliant, unique success in town. That's something to celebrate."

"Not unique for long." She wished the words back immediately. He'd want to know more about Raoul, she'd have to tell him, and he'd either tell her what to do or not see what she was worried about.

"Tell me more about that guy. Why did you have to fire him?"

Darcy sighed and told him. How Raoul had come to the restaurant in all his bad-boy sexy glory, flirted shamelessly with Darcy. She'd felt pretty hot, pretty special, until she caught him in the linen storage room with Alice. And until Ace reported missing steaks and expensive cheeses, some of which were eventually discovered in the back of Raoul's truck, where Ace had "happened" to climb to get some springtime sunshine. Ace was also a guy she could depend on. That made two. Troy might be a solid third.

When she got to the part where Raoul landed the backing

of James Thomas who'd laughed Darcy out of his office for the same request, and the details about Raoul's restaurant concept being so similar to hers, Troy went very quiet and very still.

"Doesn't play nice."

"Ya think?" She shrugged. "Nothing I can do. He's totally within his rights. No copyright on restaurant concepts, and business is business."

"It still stinks."

She nodded, waiting. He hadn't done either of the Expected Man Things, hadn't told her what to do or ignored her worries. Promising. Definitely.

"Seems to me, though, if you keep your quality up the way you're already doing, people will still come, even if he does do well. Different neighborhood, different cook. Is he any good?"

"Under me he did what he was told, to make the dishes I created. That was his job."

"Mmm, I have never tasted your food, but I do love the way you cook…" He trailed his hand down her abdomen and lower, sending a shiver of arousal through her. Again! Twice the previous evening, once in the middle of the night, already this morning. She could see why women liked younger men. "I bet you have nothing to worry about with this guy."

"I'd still like him out of the picture. Can you arrange that?"

"Sure. Um, but how about later…" His fingers started working magic between her legs. Darcy opened to him, wrapped her arms around his shoulders and welcomed him on top of her. Nothing to worry about? Hardly.

But today at least, Troy had made her feel wonderful, respected her, didn't insist on commitment, reassured her he wasn't capable of violence, didn't dismiss her fears about Raoul.…

Darcy kissed him eagerly, loving the soft insistence of his lips, the hard push of his body. She might as well face it. She'd run entirely out of reasons to resist him.

"A NEW WOMAN, HUH?"

Troy wanted to roll his eyes. He and his friend and co-worker, Chad, were on treadmills at the Milwaukee Athletic Club after work, doing their five-mile training run. He, Chad and Bev had gone to grade school together; Chad and Bev had started dating in seventh grade and never looked back, so as far as Troy was concerned, Chad had been married to Bev practically since he was born. Every time the subject was Troy's love life, the normally easygoing Chad became baffled and uptight at Troy's failure to get something so simple right the first time. "Yup. Darcy Clark. Owns Gladiolas restaurant downtown on National."

"I've heard of it." Chad grabbed his towel to mop sweat from his slightly receding hairline. "You been yet?"

"Not yet."

"What's she like?"

Troy grinned. Where to begin? "Passionate. Strong. Independent. Sexy as hell. Brunette, looks like Catherine Zeta-Jones."

"Yeah?" Chad did not sound at all impressed. But Troy wasn't out to impress him. "She old enough to drink?"

Troy shot him a look. "Since when have I ever robbed the cradle? She's thirty-two."

"Really." Chad sounded impressed that time, but Troy wasn't sure it was for good reasons. "Older woman, huh? Has she been married before?"

"Nope."

"String of failed romances?"

"Don't we all?"

Chad's gray eyes shot wide. "Uh…"

Of course not. "You're not normal, dude."

"Actually, I think I am." He pushed a button on his machine to increase the incline. Troy, ever the competitor, matched him, adjusting his stride when the running surface tilted up.

"She had a tough childhood."

"Abuse?"

"Don't think so. Alcoholic father. Sounds like her sister went down that road, too, though she's recovering. Parents had a nasty divorce."

"You want some advice?"

Troy sighed. "From you? Of course not."

"Ha-ha." Chad mopped his face again. "My advice is to stop going after these hot, flashy, unstable women. Find a nice, normal sane girl who will stay with you. Passion is great, but it doesn't last, and when it fades, you need a best friend beside you for the rest of your life."

He didn't have to ask who Chad was talking about. "Darcy isn't Debby."

"Maybe not, but she's the same type. Hot, which means men have been after her all her life. Passionate, which means emotional roller coasters all over the place. Thirty-two and never committed to anyone, baggage several feet deep from family dysfunction—it all adds up to the same story, Troy. You fall hard, then she gets bored or restless and you get hurt."

Troy drank from his water bottle, not sure how to respond to that. He had nothing to go on, no evidence handy that would convince Chad he was wrong. He hadn't known Darcy long enough to understand how she operated on every level. He was mostly going on the fact that looking into her eyes turned him upside down and inside out and beat him to a submissive pulp of tenderness and desire, which had never happened to him before to quite that degree, which he'd maybe naively assumed meant they were on their way to deeper feelings.

"How did you meet her?"

"That night you sent Justin and me to Esmee. She was at the bar, drinking arak."

"Pretty tough drink for a woman."

Troy rolled his eyes and increased the speed on his machine. "Twenty-first century, Chad."

"Right. Sorry." He punched up his speed, too, breathing slightly harder. His compact body made keeping up with Troy a battle—one he hated to lose. "Wait, I thought you were just at Esmee last week?"

"Yup. Wednesday."

"And what, she's moved in already?"

"Not exactly. We've been out twice." *The first was a chance meeting, the second she was tricked into.* That would go over great. It even sounded ridiculous to him.

"So let me get this straight. You pick this woman up at a bar, spend a couple of nights with her and now you're hooked?" Chad shook his dark head. "She's got to be something in bed. There's no other explanation for why you've turned stupid on me again after all that work getting past Drama Debby."

"That's not all it is." Troy wanted to explain further, but there was no way he was going to quote Justin's line about nerve endings coming to life.

"What can you know about a person in a week, even if you spend every second together? Bev might not be a mystery to me anymore, but it sure as hell took longer than a week to get past the initial impression." He grabbed his water bottle, took a long pull. "I was waiting until you settled after ditching Debby, but I'm thinking it's time for intervention now. Bev has a colleague at Atwood Elementary she's been wanting to match you up with, a kindergarten teacher named Jan."

Troy groaned. Chad ignored him. "She's twenty-four, smart, sweet as hell, nice family, she's great with kids, no dysfunctional garbage in her past. We'll have you over to dinner. You'll like her. Everybody likes her."

Troy wanted to laugh. He knew what was coming. *She just hasn't met the right guy yet.*

"She's dated around, but you know, she just hasn't met the right guy yet."

"Yeah?" He upped his incline, heart starting to pump; Chad swore softly and did the same. "How about that."

Maybe Troy was following his old patterns of finding women who'd treat him like crap—he and Justin used to joke about how they managed to find the psychos in every crowd. But Justin found someone sweet, sexy and devoted to him in Candy. It wasn't impossible that Troy had changed, too.

"Can I tell Bev you're interested?"

"Chad…"

"All you have to do is meet her, not propose."

"I know." He gritted his teeth. There was no way he could fit another woman in his brain right now. But if he said no, Chad would keep pestering, if for no other reason than Bev would keep pestering him. "I need to see where this goes first."

"I already know where it's going."

Troy responded by increasing his speed to a sprint. Chad followed, and they did the last quarter mile in a mess of sloppy form and heaving chests before they stopped, out of breath and laughing.

Before Chad could start in again, Troy changed the subject to Packers football and their playoff odds for the next season, counting on the topic to take over Chad's football-addicted brain completely, relieved when it worked all the way through their cool-down walk and into the weight room, where Chad did a perfunctory set and went home to Bev.

Troy stayed, working hard, then harder, working out muscles in his body and working out issues in his brain. Darcy during bicep curls. Jan during chest presses. Darcy during pec flies. His old girlfriend Debby during triceps kickbacks. Darcy during sit-ups on the slant board. Where was he messing up? Where were the women messing up?

He pictured Bev, Chad's wife, her peaceful smile, her welcoming home, the constancy of her attention and devotion to her husband.

Troy would be bored to death.

He sat up the last time, grinning. To death. He'd come home to Jan who had a hot dinner waiting, smiling welcome, and he'd just dissolve into a puddle of boredom and cease to be.

Whereas Darcy... Coming home to her... Now that would be a *hot* dinner.

He got off the slant board and down to the showers before his shorts took on a peculiar shape.

Troy had learned his lesson dating Debby. He wouldn't make the same mistakes again. But that didn't mean he had to go in the opposite direction and set a life course with Donna Reed.

He wanted Darcy, to the exclusion of any other type of woman he could imagine. There was no point trying to drive himself crazy going against his instinct.

The only trick going forward was to make sure Darcy kept wanting him.

9

MARIE WAS NEARLY READY. OH, MY Lord, nearly ready and shaking from nerves, and furious with herself for being at all anxious. How many times had she been out alone with Quinn? Practically every week since they'd officially introduced themselves in January, five months ago at the Roots Restaurant and Cellar bar. When had he ever been anything more than an easy, comfortable companion? Just because they were going to be meeting at a different restaurant didn't mean anything else would change.

Except he'd never asked Marie to a place this fancy before. And he'd never asked Marie out dancing. And Marie had never been this close to admitting to him how deeply she felt.

She stalked over to her full-length mirror. Yeah, admit that she was in love with him and watch him recoil in horror. She reminded him of his sister, right? Angela. Which was ridiculous, because Marie had met Angela. She was slender, dark and lovely. Marie was short, plump and...

Hmm. She couldn't help grinning at her reflection. Funny that she'd be thinking of Angela because the first time Marie saw Quinn's sister, Marie had been wearing this dress in a doomed attempt to get Quinn to notice her sexually. She'd shown up at Roots, decked out in this blow-him-away finery, and had seen Quinn with his arm around a beautiful woman. Assuming he was in the midst of a seduction, Marie had turned tail and run, unnecessarily devastated.

Silver lining—Quinn still hadn't seen her in this dress, which would be perfect for tonight. And yes, she still looked wonderful in it. The white cotton knit bodice criss-crossed over her generous breasts, giving him more of an eyeful than she was used to showing, but inflicting maximum cleavage on people seemed to be the style now, so why not?

Under her breasts, a band of solid blue, then a cascade of blue lining and a blue-green floral overskirt to just below her knees. The dress worked. It slimmed her, complemented the auburn shade she'd chosen for her hair, and made her skin look fresh and alive, bringing out good colors in her hazel eyes. Add the miraculously easy-to-walk-in blue heels and matching purse, and she was dressed to kill in a way Quinn had never seen. He'd better react.

Another look, turning this-way and that-way, enjoying the swirling folds of fabric. Would she be the sexiest woman there? Not by a long shot. Would she be the most beautiful? Ha! Not even close. But did she look about as good as she could? Absolutely. Which was all she wanted tonight.

Um, okay, that was a bald lie. She wanted a hell of a lot more than that tonight. When she opened the door to Quinn, she wanted his eyes to widen in astonishment, then narrow with lust. She wanted him to take her arm possessively, use any excuse to touch her, growl at other men who might glance her way, hold her too close while they were dancing, and leave early to get her into his bed where he'd declare undying passion before making love to her with every part of his body and his heart and his—

Wake up, Marie! Back to reality. Tonight she'd be thrilled with attentiveness, admiration and the pleasure of his company. She did not want to set herself up for feeling the evening was anything but a huge success.

One step forward and she examined her makeup more closely in the mirror. Maybe a touch more of the blue-green liner around the corner of her eyes, though excitement had made them large and shining. So maybe she'd—

Her phone rang; she crushed down the dread that it was Quinn calling to cancel. No negative thoughts tonight. None. Everything low-key and calm. That was the only way she'd get through this intact.

"Hey, it's Kim."

"Kim, hi, how's it going?" She grinned at her reflection. The date would go on.

"Everything is going great! Nathan got a job with a local firm specializing in green architecture. We were on our way to meet with the caterer and he just got called."

"How fabulous!" Marie's shriek startled her gray tabby, Jezebel, who'd been sleeping on the bed. She gave Marie a withering look and settled back down. "I'm so happy for both of you."

"Yes, it's wonderful. He starts next week. It's done a lot for him."

"I can imagine." Marie gave a secret smile. Nathan had done some impressive growing up in the last few months. "And what about your job? How is the Carter website coming along? They liking your designs?"

"Loving them. The bureaucracy is making me want to tear my hair out, but artistically it's really satisfying."

"I am thrilled for you, Kim. Sounds like life is shaping up."

"It's pretty great. I'm calling also because Candy's crazy busy this week, but she wants to set up a meeting with Darcy to go over the Milwaukeedates party plans she emailed you, look at menus, and so on. We wondered if Monday at 10:00 a.m. would work for you?"

"Hang on." She went over to her bag, dug out her iPhone. "The seventh? Looks fine."

"Good, I'll let Candy and Darcy know. Thanks. Are you relaxing tonight?"

"No. I'm going out." She couldn't stop the smile.

"Really? With whom?"

"A friend."

"Quinn!"

Marie started. "How did you know?"

"You sound so happy. Is this a date? Where are you going?"

"Dream Dance. And I'm not sure."

"Dream Dance?" She sounded as if she was going to have an apoplectic fit. "And you're not *sure? * Marie, men don't take women there as friends. Trust me on this."

"I'm not—"

"Nathan is nodding like crazy. He says coffee dates for friends. Dream Dance for girlfriends."

"You are not helping."

"What do you mean?"

"The only way I'm going to get through this night is not to think that—"

Doorbell. Invasion of serious nerves.

"Oh, my God. He's here. I have to go."

"Have fun! Call and tell us all about it."

Marie groaned. Kim would tell Candy, Candy would tell Darcy, they'd be wondering all night what was happening. Like she needed this pressure?

No. No, Marie Hewitt was stronger than this. Marie Hewitt had survived infidelity and divorce, and had started her own successful business out of nothing. Marie Hewitt could get through a date.

She stood tall, eyes closed, body centered, and took two deep, calming breaths.

There. Marie Hewitt was ready.

She picked up the blue purse and matching light jacket, hoping it would be enough to keep her warm in this cool weather, and forced herself to walk with calm dignity down the stairs, for her own peace of mind and so she wouldn't trip and end their date in the emergency room before it even began.

The bell rang again. Oh, impatient man. If only he were that impatient for her, and not just results.

She put on a smile and opened the door, making sure her expression was friendly and casual, because it would be pretty pathetic to greet him with all the anxiety and hope she was feeling.

The smile, however, dropped. Quinn stood there, the epitome of magnetic masculine success in a charcoal suit that fit flawlessly over his broad shoulders, and over a white shirt and classic burgundy-and-blue tie. He was freshly shaved and smelled incredibly sexy. For a too-long moment she was overwhelmed, then forced herself to put her tongue back into her mouth, figuratively speaking, and collect herself.

"Hi, Quinn." She managed to focus properly and noticed with a tiny kick of excitement that he seemed a little dazed himself.

"Marie." He gestured to her dress. "You look…stunning. Beautiful."

"Oh, hey, thanks. You do, too." She threw out the words, nonchalance personified, turned to lock the door behind her and let a full grin have its way as soon as her face was safely hidden. She'd worship this dress for the rest of her life, build a shrine and leave money for its preservation in her will. "I'm looking forward to the evening."

"Same here." His low, deep voice made her shiver and her

resolve to be cool faltered again. She had a feeling the entire evening was going to a series of similar battles.

Bring it on.

They drove to Dream Dance, located in the Potawatomi Casino, southwest of downtown Milwaukee in the Menomonee River Valley, a fortress of a building with four towers topped with round dishes containing leaping orange flames, a dramatic statement in the dark even with the copious lighting around the stark stone walls.

Quinn turned his silver Lexus sedan over to valet parking and gallantly escorted Marie through what seemed a random door, but which turned out to be conveniently opposite the restaurant entrance. Did he ever miss a beat? Stumble? Look like a dork? It would actually make her feel better. Maybe she should steal his wallet so he'd be caught thinking he had no money to pay for the meal.

They pushed through the doors and over a short tiled hallway into the restaurant's foyer, where they were greeted and welcomed into the dining room, whose white-clothed tables sat widely spaced for privacy. Marie and Quinn were shown to a table embraced by a semicircular high-backed banquette on which she and Quinn sat next to each other and faced the room. The noise was low, waiters moved around leisurely attending the well-dressed patrons. Marie felt like royalty.

"Do you come here often, Quinn?"

"Not very." He turned slightly so he could face her. "Have you been here before?"

"Oh, sure, once a week at least." She sent him an acerbic glance that made him chuckle.

"I've been here a few times. Always had excellent meals. But my theory is that if you do special-occasion things too frequently, they lose some of their magic."

"I agree." She hated that she was already wondering what woman he'd been here with and how special she was to him.

"I've only been here with clients. This is my first social visit."

Had he read her mind? The violent blush threatening to climb up her face would have been humiliating if the waiter hadn't chosen that moment to introduce himself, welcome them, hand them menus, Quinn a wine list, and suggest drinks.

Quinn quirked an eyebrow in her direction. "Champagne?"

Marie smiled sweetly, as if she was offered the stuff every day, wondering how much a bottle went for in a place like this, then deciding she didn't want to know. "Can anyone say no to champagne?"

"Not anyone I'd like to know." He turned back to the waiter and pointed to the wine list. "How about a bottle of the Perrier Jouët?"

"Certainly." The waiter nodded politely and strode off.

"Are we celebrating something?" Marie asked.

"Of course."

"What?"

"Hmm." He looked pensive. "I give up. Do we need a reason?"

Marie laughed. *How about the deep love that you're about to confess you feel for me?* "Not at all."

Another server came by with a crystal tulip glass for each of them and a footed metal bucket to keep the champagne cold, draped with a white linen towel. Marie couldn't stop smiling. Everything about the place felt luxurious, relaxing and totally indulgent, from the soft cushioned back of their banquette to the small light hanging over their table dripping sparkling crystals, to the bevy of waiters working to make them comfortable and satisfied. But she'd probably feel pampered and indulged in a cafeteria with Quinn, too. Every second in his presence felt like a special event.

"So how goes your matchmaking with Darcy?"

She regarded him suspiciously. "Do you really want to know or are you going to lecture me again?"

"Lecture?" He put his hand to his chest, the picture of wounded innocence. "Is that what I did?"

"Um, yeah?"

He dropped the act, gave a genuine smile. "Marie, I have tremendous respect for you, even if I don't love all your methods. If I lectured, I'm sorry."

"It's fine." She put her hand on his forearm, and wanted to leave it there. She got the chance when he covered her hand with his and squeezed, making it very difficult for her to keep her mind on what she wanted to say. "As for matchmaking, I assume it went well, because Darcy hasn't called to scream at me again and it's been three days."

Quinn lifted his brows. "From what you said, she's the type who'd have no problem screaming if she thought she was entitled."

"Not the slightest. But I haven't heard a word, which I'm daring to hope is because she's embarrassed it worked, rather than so furious she's not speaking to me."

"Any way you can find out?"

"I could…" Marie made a face. "A roundabout way, through Justin and Candy and Troy. But believe it or not I'm trying to respect her privacy."

"What?" Quinn faked convincing shock. "When did you come up with that novel idea?"

"Ha…ha."

The waiter returned with the champagne in a green bottle with gold foil, hand-painted with a spray of white flowers. He removed the cork with a discreet *thunk,* and poured an inch for Quinn to try. On approval, he poured cold bubbly magic for each of them and nestled the bottle into the ice bucket.

"Cheers, Marie." Quinn lifted his glass. "Here's to us.

To the past few months of friendship and to the rest of our lives."

"Hear, hear." She clinked, smiled and sipped, thrilled by the "rest of their lives" concept, determinedly refusing to listen to the little voice repeating Kim and Nathan's opinion about men taking women to Dream Dance. Marie could do a lot worse than be friends with this man for the rest of her life, and that was going to be the focus from now on or she'd implode from anxiety.

"Tell me something, Marie."

"If you ask maybe I will."

"If money and time were no object, where would you most like to go in the world?"

"Oh, I love this kind of question. It always fits my budget." She put her champagne down and clasped her hands under her chin. "Sydney. No, London. No, Paris. No, all three."

"Really?" His eyes were amused. "Not some tropical resort?"

"No, no." She waved the idea away. "If I'm spending imaginary time and money, I want to see the world, not lie on a beach. Though it's not like I'd fight to leave a tropical resort if I landed there."

"Gotcha."

"What about you?"

"Sydney, London and Paris sound perfect."

"So—" Marie lifted her shoulder in a nonchalant shrug "—when do we leave?"

Quinn chuckled and lifted his glass for another clink. "Next month. This one is busy for me."

"July." She clinked and drank rapturously, loving the fizz of bubbles on her tongue and the clear, smooth taste.

"You know where else I want to go? To Gladiolas. Darcy promised us a meal. I say we take her up on it."

"Oh, yes, the food there is wonderful." Marie patted her

stomach rapturously. "Her menu ideas and titles are so cre-
ative and funny. People really enjoy them. Though if her
ex-employee Raoul has his way, she won't be so original
anymore."

"What's that about?"

She told him the gist, tickled when he responded with
anger. Protective men got her juices running. That he was
protective not only of her but of her friend...

"Women have it tough in the restaurant business. A lot of
prejudices. Classic case of having to work twice as hard to be
considered half as good." He looked thoughtfully at the table,
moving his silverware back and forth. Marie waited patiently,
happy to admire the sexy gray touching his temple, and the
fine line of his smooth-shaven jaw.

"That's double reason we should go, then." He looked up,
features set in resolve, and she had to look down at her own
silverware, because sometimes he was just too sexy for her
to handle without disgracing herself. "I'll do some investigat-
ing. Maybe I can put some money into Gladiolas and help her
compete if it comes to that."

Marie's eyes shot wide. "You'd do that for her?"

"And for you. But also for business. The restaurant would
have to be a good risk."

"Of course." She drank champagne, drank more, moved
beyond anything she wanted to show him. Talk about a knight
in shining armor. "When did you want to go?"

"This week." He hauled out his iPhone; she dutifully hauled
out hers, giddy from champagne and Dream Dance and Quinn.
This week? She was seeing him tonight, then again at Gladiolas, then Saturday for their Chicago trip...

They made a tentative plan for the following Wednesday.
The waiter refilled their glasses. And again. The rest of the
champagne disappeared leisurely, accompanying an appetizer
of yellowfin tuna that was out of this world. With Quinn's

steak and Marie's lamb tenderloin, they shared a bottle of exceptional Bordeaux from Chateau Mouton-Rothschild, which probably cost more than Marie's entire outfit. But oh, it was something. Dry, smooth and delicious not only with the meat, but with the selection of Wisconsin cheeses that followed the entrée. By that time Marie was feeling no pain, but considerable smug satisfaction that her dress wasn't tight. For dessert they split a fruit sorbet and had coffee, Quinn paid and they staggered to the restaurant exit.

"Still feel like dancing?"

"I don't think it matters what I feel like. I need to dance. What was that, about a week's worth of calories?"

"What do you care?" He grabbed her hand to steer her past a boisterous bunch entering the building, and didn't let go.

"I care because I shouldn't gain any more weight." She adjusted her fingers in his, loving the warm secure contact and, speaking of warm, was it her imagination or had the temperature actually risen from damp chill to less-damp chill while they were eating?

"No. Don't gain. Or lose." Quinn sent her the sexiest sidelong glance any woman had ever had the pleasure of receiving. "You're perfect."

Marie rolled her eyes. "You are too used to flattering women. How will we ever know if you're telling the truth when it counts?"

He stopped walking; her momentum took her a couple of steps past. He tugged her around until she was facing him. His hands landed on her shoulders. "Marie."

"Yuh."

"Listen to me. You are an attractive woman. And smart and funny and sexy. That is my sincere opinion and I'm sure the opinion of many other men. It is not flattery. Okay?"

Marie stood stupidly, chin hanging down in surprise. "I. Well."

He looked exasperated. "Just say, 'Yes, Quinn, I am all those things.'"

"Yes, Quinn." She spoke demurely, then burst into giggles from sheer happiness. Was there another man this wonderful anywhere else?

"Promise me, no more beating yourself up." He glanced to the side where a car had pulled up to the walk. "Here we go."

The driver got out, opened the back door and stood waiting. Back door?

Marie followed Quinn, surprised when he gestured her in and joined her. "You're not driving?"

"After we killed off two bottles of wine? No, thanks."

Marie looked at him incredulously. "Dream Dance provides designated drivers?"

"Nope." He grinned. "I do."

She laughed, not because she thought the idea was at all funny, but because when he smiled at her like that, with such warmth and mischief in his eyes, she couldn't help it.

They were driven to The Jazz House in the Third Ward and dropped off to catch the last hour of the band. Marie loved to dance, had taken lessons as a kid on her mother's insistence, but never found a decent partner. She and her ex, Grant, had danced at their own wedding, and a couple of times at other people's, and that was it.

Of course, of *course,* Quinn was a superb dancer, stylish, inventive and easy to follow. They took frequent breaks for big glasses of water and conversation. She hadn't ever had so much fun with a guy. Ever.

By the time the band slowed for the final dance, she was feeling giddy, but less affected by the wine, with a clearer head. She went into Quinn's arms, comfortable with their easy friendship and enjoying his warmth and solidity, the smooth sway of their bodies, chaste inches apart.

"Marie."

"Mmm?"

"Will you go dancing with me again sometime?"

"Anytime," she murmured.

"Good." He pulled her closer, then loosened his hold, too soon for her taste. "I think you're my favorite person to spend time with."

"You're mine, too."

"Yeah?" He looked down at her.

Marie met his eyes without hesitation. "Yeah."

The moment was perfect for a first kiss. The atmosphere, the dialogue, the way her lips tingled in instinctive anticipation, everything pointed that way. But this was Quinn, and their first kiss would never happen. For the first time she thought she felt truly at peace with that. Totally comfortable and able to be straight with him. On everything except being in love. "So tell me, Quinn."

"Mmm?"

"What happens to us when you get that girlfriend you're looking for?"

His expression changed. "I'm…not sure how to answer that, Marie."

"Okay. I guess I'm going to put it right out there that I will be devastated if you leave me for someone else." She strove for a light tone and to keep smiling, and managed both. Good for her. She was really doing this.

"Then how about I don't leave you?"

Marie giggled. "Somehow I can't see you happy with only a platonic relationship in your life."

"No. I couldn't do that." His speech had become clipped. Maybe it was better to drop the topic. She'd made it clear how she felt—up to a point. She wasn't going to put him in the horrible position of admitting that she'd be stuck on the back burner when he found his Miss Perfect. All she could hope was that it would take him the next fifty years to find her. In the meantime, evenings spent with this god of a man would go a long way toward making her own life special until she got to the point where she could entertain starting a relationship of her own with a mere mortal.

The band broke for the evening. After restroom visits, they piled into Quinn's chauffeur-driven Lexus and headed back to Brewer's Hill, stopping first at Marie's house, which looked dark and anticlimactic after the evening of glitz and glamor. Still, it was where she belonged. Jezebel would greet her, she'd get back to planning the party with Candy, Kim and Darcy and the rest of her rich, full life would go happily on. What had Quinn said? Something to the effect that doing anything special too often made it less special. She wasn't sure going out with him could ever feel ordinary, but maybe it could. And she already had Gladiolas midweek and next Saturday in Chicago to look forward to with him.

With that delicious thought in mind, she nearly took Quinn out by determinedly shoving open her door, not realizing he'd come around to open it for her. "Sorry."

"It's fine. You missed me. I'll walk you to your door."

"You are so gallant." She took his offered hand and got out of the car. "This was about the most wonderful and romantic evening of my entire life."

"Romantic?"

She cringed. Did he have to get all defensive like that? "Champagne, fabulous food and service, dancing…what could be more romantic?"

"Yes, well…" He followed her to her door, waited while she dug out her keys. "I had a wonderful time too, Marie."

She turned and smiled brightly. "Good."

"You're still game for Chicago next weekend on top of dinner at Gladiolas?"

"Absolutely."

"Good. Because I'm looking forward to spending more time with you." He took her shoulders and leaned in; she puckered for a friendly good-night peck.

Instead, his mouth was soft meeting her tight lips, which went slack with surprise. He lingered, lighting sparklers all the way down inside her.

This was not a friendly peck. It was a kiss. A real one. *Quinn was kissing her.*

She was still trying to wrap her brain around that concept when he pulled back, brushed her bangs tenderly off her forehead, and leaned in again for another briefer but just as sweet meeting of their lips. "Good night. Sleep well. I'll call you tomorrow."

"Yes. You, too. Sure!" She wanted to sound husky and sexual, but her voice came out all nervous and chirpy. Had she gone into shock? Maybe it had been too many months assuming Quinn felt nothing, so now she couldn't act any other way. "You know me! I'll be around!"

For God's sake, stop twittering, Marie.

He looked disconcerted and backed away, sexy frown between his brows. "Yeah. Okay. Good night."

"G'night." She went inside, feeling slightly hysterical. He'd kissed her. *He'd kissed her.* What did that mean? Did he have feelings? Did he…

She threw her blue purse on her couch, kicked off her heels and stalked around her living room, muttering and gesturing in disgust.

Enough. *Enough.*

This was absolutely ridiculous. She'd spent a ridiculous amount of time tiptoeing around Quinn and her feelings.

Gladiolas would be too public, territory inhabited by people who knew her. But next Saturday she was going to tell this man the truth, a truth she'd owed him for some weeks now, a truth that could either cement them together or break them forever apart.

She was absolutely crazy in love with him.

10

DARCY BURST INTO THE GLADIOLAS kitchen, shivering and dripping from rain she hadn't expected, annoyed at arriving later than she'd wanted to. Especially because they had a wedding rehearsal dinner that night for twenty-five people. She'd slept late and then hadn't been able to summon her usual focus to get the house and kitchen ready for her and Troy's date that night.

But what else was new? Since they'd met two and a half weeks ago, she'd barely been able to focus on anything but him. Things between them were going too well. Maybe she just wasn't used to relationships that weren't toxic, but she couldn't help feeling some poop would have to hit some fan sometime soon. She wasn't accustomed to being so happy, found she couldn't trust the feeling or relax completely into it. When she was with him, everything was fine. On her own, the dark fears surfaced and played rounds of racquetball with her brain.

When she'd been dating Jon, her boyfriend in college, and Chris, her boyfriend after, she'd been constantly coming up against issues, constantly aware of the problems and the ways they didn't fit each other, all the danger signs of controlling and selfish behavior, so familiar from growing up with her father.

So far, being with Troy was simply blissful fun. If there were any unhealthy patterns, she had yet to see them.

Her staff was already at work, sous chef Sean, assistant Ben and dishwasher Ace preparing for a busy day, the heavy metal music she couldn't abide blasting from the battered CD player perched on the counter. As soon as Ace saw her, he headed for the machine.

"No, no." She waved him away. "Leave it. It's fine."

Ace blinked in surprise and shot a glance at Sean. Darcy took a few more steps and stopped at the sight of a plate of food at Ace's station. "What's this?"

Ace looked guilty. "Lunch."

"Can I try?"

Another glance at Sean and he grabbed a spoon and tossed it to her. "Sure."

Darcy scooped up some of the fish in a smooth dark orange sauce. The flavors burst onto her tongue—cardamom, garlic, red chili and peanut? She turned to Sean. "Who made this?"

Sean pointed behind her.

Darcy whirled around to stare at Ace. "You made this."

"Yup."

"Someone's recipe?"

Ace shook his head, tapping his temple. "From here."

She spooned up more to taste again. Complex layers of flavor, just enough heat, a little too much spice for such a delicate fish, but impressive nonetheless. "Ace, come into my office."

"Uh, sure." He ambled after her, stayed on his feet as the door closed, looking wary as hell. "Look, chef, I was just—"

"Sit." She gestured to the metal folding chair set up on the other side of her desk.

He sat, rubbing his hands nervously along his thighs.

"The restaurant is doing well. We could use help. I've been thinking about having you on the line more often, Ace. I see a lot of potential in you, a lot of creativity. You're good with a knife and you're good with flavors. I've seen you quietly correcting dishes when Sean gets sloppy, which he does too often. I think you could have a decent career in this business if that's what you wanted."

His blue eyes opened wider than she'd seen them in quite a while, if ever. "Really?"

"Yeah, really." She leaned forward, folding her hands onto her desk on top of a pile of bills, wondering what had taken her so long to do this for him. "I'd like to help you, but there is one condition."

Wary again. Big-time. His surprisingly delicate brows gathered. "What's that?"

"On days you work the line in my kitchen, you come to work clean." She held his gaze, watching the wheels turning… slowly…in his chemically altered brain.

"Clean."

"I did it. It's possible."

"You?"

She nodded impatiently, not about to share more of her past with this kid. "Can you do it?"

"Well…yeah." The word came out uncertainly. *C'mon, Ace.* He frowned and then his face cleared. "Yeah. I can do that."

"Good." She banged her palm on the desk, feeling more emotional than she expected to. She liked Ace; she wanted to help him. And it was wonderful to be in a position where she could do what chef Paul had done for her. "I'll hold you to it. Now. We have a party tonight. Get out there and work."

"Yes, ma'am." He got halfway to the door, which was all of a single step, and turned back. "Thanks, chef."

"Just don't screw up." She smiled at him.

"You should do that more often."

"Tell you to get off drugs?"

"Smile. It makes you look human. And your aura is amazing today. Has been for the last two weeks."

She rolled her eyes and pointed to the door. "Out."

Yes, okay, she was in a good mood. No, a great one. And she didn't have to look far to know what was causing it. She hadn't felt like this in so long. Actually, she'd never felt like this. Happy, yes, giddy in love, yes, but this time…she suspected that Troy would be someone she could lean on. Someone who just might go the extra mile to support her, instead of wondering only what she could do for him. Was that possible?

No, she didn't hate all men, only the type she'd always attracted. No, she wasn't against relationships, just the self-destructive, soul-depleting ones she'd always had.

Not hard to see why.

This man…of course it was ridiculously early. They'd spent only a few weeks together, but the way he spoke to her, the way he respected her talent and seemed to respect her devotion to her career, never harping on all the time she spent away from him. His confidence in her ability to withstand the Raoul copycat restaurant warmed her, even if she didn't think he was right.

In short, today, she was full of the joyous bloom of love for humanity, for herself, for everyone. Could this last? Of course not. Every couple started out this way, putting best feet forward. Sooner or later the cracks would inevitably show. It was just that for the first time she had real hope the cracks would stay cracks, and not turn into enormous fissures that widened until they swallowed her completely.

Her phone rang. "Gladiolas, Chef Darcy Clark speaking."

"Hey."

Her professional face melted into a smile that Ace would probably say made her superhuman. "Troy. What's up?"

"Wondered if there was anything you wanted me to bring tonight."

"Not a thing. What are you doing?"

"About to go over to the club to work out. Everything going well there today?"

"Very." She tipped her head back, rested it on the back of her chair. "The staff is confused, though."

"Why's that? Because it's freezing in June?"

"No, but it is. I'm having to delay our usual transition to hot weather food. Last night's special was called June is the New March."

"So why is your staff confused?"

Darcy smirked. "They seem to think I'm becoming human."

"Really." He sounded distinctly amused. "How strange. Why do you think that is?"

"I have no idea. They've certainly never thought I was before."

"Hmm. Anything new in your life?"

"Well…" She ran her hands over her breasts, imagining Troy's touch. "I do have this new young lover. Very hot."

"Mmm. Tell me more. Because I have a really hot lover, too."

"Ooh." She brushed her hand between her legs, becoming aroused just talking to him. "Re-e-ally hot?"

"Yes-s-s. Hot to look at. Hot to sleep with. Hot to touch." His slow, deep voice was turning her into jelly. "Sometimes I'm afraid I'll get burned."

Darcy caught her breath. Her hand stilled. She couldn't

tell if he was serious or kidding, but she knew exactly what he meant. "Maybe you should invest in asbestos gloves."

"I hope I won't have to, Darcy."

"Yes." She wanted to reassure him, tell him in a firm voice that she wouldn't ever hurt him, but the words wouldn't come. Who knew what lay ahead? She didn't want to be hurt, either, but you couldn't plan for that future, no matter how wonderful the present felt. Just ask her parents.

"Tell me more about your day, Darcy."

"Let's see." She switched gears along with him, enjoying the simple pleasure of sharing life's more mundane details with him. "I talked to Ace just now about assuming more responsibility once he's clean. I think he'll make an effort at least. Actually, no, I think he'll do it."

"Good. Good for you, Darcy." His enthusiasm made her wonder if he was thinking of his brother, Tom, lost to drugs in a way she hoped Ace never would. "No more harassment from Raoul?"

"None."

"I'd say you're having a good day."

She pitched her voice seductively low. "I'd say it will get much better when it turns to night."

"Mmm. You keep saying things like that and I'll come over right now and take you over your desk."

"Oooh." She fanned herself. "You're right, I'd better be careful. Because that would be entirely wonderful."

Troy laughed. "See you later, Darcy."

"Don't work out too hard. I'll need those muscles all night long."

"I promise." He ended the call; Darcy hung up and stretched luxuriously, lifting her hair off the back of her neck and letting it spill down. Could she be any more of a cliché? Probably not. She loved that he called to ask about her day, seemed to care about what was going on with her as well as to report in on what was going on with him. Loved hearing his voice, loved that he liked her enough to be able to think about her once in a while.

The phone rang again; she reached languorously for the receiver. "Gladiolas, Chef Darcy."

"Darce-y."

"Raoul." Speak of the devil. She rolled her eyes, miraculously not more than mildly annoyed to hear from him. Was this in fact what it felt like to be human? "How the hell are you?"

"Now that I'm talking to you? Wonderful."

"Uh-huh." Darcy leaned back in her chair, making a gagging motion. From Troy to Mr. Snake Oil Salesman. But it said a lot that even his creepy charm hadn't been able to obliterate her bliss. At least not yet. "What can I do for you, Raoul? We're busy today."

"I knew that. Just wanted to let you know that I'm a friend of your groom."

"My what?" Darcy started. He knew Troy?

"The rehearsal dinner tonight at Gladiolas. I know the groom."

"Oh. Right. Gotcha." Her face flamed. Not Troy. Jeez, where was her mind going?

"I wanted to warn you so you wouldn't freak out when I showed up. I know I'm not your favorite person these days."

"Nope." She bit her lip. That was actually fairly decent of him to warn her. Maybe Troy was right and she'd been over-reacting. Hurting herself more than she hurt him by being so angry and bitter. Maybe Troy was exactly the emotional balance she'd been thinking she needed for a while. "I appreciate the advance notice. Truth is we'll be so busy I probably would barely have seen you."

"Yeah, I know all about that. Everything in ship shape?"

She made a face at the receiver. No, Raoul, they were all

experienced professionals, but it hadn't occurred to them to make any preparations.

"We have a good crew, you know that. We're ready."

"What's for dinner?"

Everything open and warm inside Darcy slammed shut and froze. None of his damn business what her menus were.

She closed her eyes. *Come on, Darcy.* He was coming that night for dinner, he'd find out anyway. "Pea-zucchini soup with thyme, chicken with bacon, leeks and rosemary and hazelnut chocolate chunk cake for dessert."

"Oh, yeah, you have the touch. I'm looking forward to being at the old place, Darcy. Look forward to seeing everyone." He took a quick breath as if he were going to speak, then stopped. "I, uh, I'm sorry if I've been an ass."

Darcy snorted, but she was surprised by the sincerity in his voice. "You can't help it, Raoul. It's what you are."

He laughed, and for one second she felt again the camaraderie they'd had—she thought they'd had—as chef and sous chef, before she found out his true colors.

"See you tonight, honey."

She sighed loudly, mouth twisting into a reluctant grin. "If it can't be avoided, yeah, I guess I will."

He hung up, chuckling, and she hung up, face hot, feeling triumphant. Troy had been right. Acting as if she couldn't care if he lived or died was much less damaging than being actively hostile. She couldn't do anything about his restaurant—he had every right to open it, so she could either let it eat her up and destroy her peace and sanity or she could accept it and keep enjoying running Gladiolas.

She stretched her arms up again, thinking of Troy's handsome face, his body taut over hers, the fierce desire registering in his face before he reached his climax and slumped over into tenderness and sweet caresses.

Oh, the way he touched her…

A darkening at her door wiped the dreamy smile off her lips in a big hurry. Amy, holding her ubiquitous cup of coffee in one hand and a paper in the other. Darcy beckoned her in. "Hey, what's going on?"

"Just wanted to confirm that salad is being served *after* the entrée tonight."

"Yes, that's how they wanted it."

"Good." Amy slid the paper onto Darcy's desk, looking at her curiously. "Candy called earlier this morning. She said having the next planning session for the Milwaukeedates party would work fine at your usual Women in Power meeting. She chose this menu preliminarily."

"Good, thanks." Darcy skimmed the menu. Mostly finger foods, nothing exotic or too complicated. They had most of the ingredients and could easily order the rest in time. "How are things with Colin? Is he behaving?"

"He is. I'm crazy about this guy." She patted her heart. "And ridiculously hopeful. And ridiculously terrified."

Darcy put the menu into her upright file. Yeah, she got that. All too well. "Things do work out. Maybe this guy is right for you."

Amy narrowed her eyes over her mug. "They're right."

"Who?" Darcy looked up sharply. "About what?"

"You. You're different."

"Me?" Darcy put her hand to her chest, doing her best to sound incredulous. "Different?"

"Mmm-hmm." Amy perched on the edge of Darcy's desk. "There's a rumor going around, both kitchen and dining-room staff."

"Rumor? About what?"

"You."

Darcy narrowed her eyes. "Okay, let's have it."

"Apparently big, tough, invincible Chef Darcy…" She broke

off to examine her nails as if they were the most fascinating things in the room.

"What?"

Amy looked up, blinking in fake surprise. "Oh, did I not mention it? Silly me."

Darcy growled. "A-*my*."

She did a bad job suppressing her trademark waterfall of giggles and leaned forward conspiratorially. "They say Chef Darcy has fallen in love."

DARCY OPENED HER FRONT DOOR, arms full, damp from the rain. On her way out that morning, she'd taken a look around her house through a stranger's eyes, thinking of Troy there that evening, and had been dismayed by how bare-walled and sterile the place looked. Coming home, she'd passed by her favorite independent bookstore, which had been featuring an irresistible vibrantly colored series of framed food prints in the window: fruits, vegetables, cheeses, cakes, pastries—she'd ducked in and bought them all. At the supermarket where she'd gotten last-minute ingredients for Troy's favorite meal, she'd added to her cart three generic but cheerful mixed bouquets of flowers.

Troy was coming over after his workout; she expected him about nine, which gave her an hour to cook and redecorate.

The meal was the easy part. She remembered exactly what he'd said were his favorites: burger, medium rare, on a sesame roll with a slice of tomato, sweet onion, lettuce, pickle, catsup and mustard, French fries, coleslaw and ice-cold beer. For dessert, chocolate milkshake. In the interest of time, she'd gotten the French fries from a burger joint, but the hamburgers would be made from beef raised at her favorite local farm, the sesame buns fresh from a nearby bakery, the coleslaw homemade and the chocolate to flavor the shake was from Ghana, sixty percent cacao.

Entice Your Man Burger, with Flirty Fries and a Shimmy Shake.

She bustled around the kitchen preparing the hamburgers, flavored with salt, porcini mushroom powder and plenty of pepper, slicing tomato, onion and pickle, tossing the French fries with herbed parmesan cheese to reheat later, shredding cabbage, mixing the dressing and adding cream to the melted chocolate for the milkshake flavoring.

After setting the dining table with her nice blue-rimmed plates and pilsner glasses for the beer, Darcy glanced at the clock. Half an hour. She took a lightning-speed shower, yanked on form-fitting black knit pants and a hot pink sweater, threw on makeup.

Now. Twenty minutes to transform the apartment. *Please let him be late.* Darcy dragged a chair over to the refrigerator and stood to reach into a cabinet above for vases. Holding three, she stepped down gingerly, hopping to maintain balance on the landing like an Olympic gymnast, ran water into each, yanked the plastic off the bouquets and stuffed them in.

One on the counter by the window. One on the table where they'd eat. One…she frowned, then ran into her living room and set them on one end of the coffee table, not in the center as was her instinct. She pulled a couple of books out of the bookshelf and scattered them next to the vase, then dashed into her room, grabbed her slippers, neatly stowed under the bed, and tossed them at the foot of the wingback chair by the fire.

Good.

Posters next. She ran to her supply closet, found a hammer and a rarely used assortment of nails she'd gotten five years ago from the hardware store when she bought the house, a pencil and a measuring tape. In fifteen minutes she'd hung all but one, maybe not perfectly aligned, but not terrible.

Troy was due in five minutes. Maybe he'd help her hang the last one?

In her bedroom, she grimaced at the perfect order, scattered mail across the bare desk, then spilled out a couple of pens from her supply neatly stashed in a mug that said, "Before you tell a man you love his company, make sure he owns one."

Wait. Again into the kitchen, she got a glass from the cabinet, filled it with an inch of water, raced back and put it on her desk. Better. Could she stand leaving socks on the floor?

No. Darcy had to draw the line somewhere.

At her bedroom door, she surveyed the intentional damage to the house. Much better. The posters added perfect color; her red slippers made a casual statement in the living room. The plates of food on the kitchen counter, and the few dishes in the sink added even more.

Ace would be proud. Now her house looked "human," too. He'd given her another look of astonishment that evening when Raoul had come swaggering back into the kitchen to say hello, and Darcy had managed to fight down bile and be fairly gracious. Or at least she hadn't slugged him when he managed a few veiled insults to their location and chances of making a big success, and bragged that his restaurant would be called Raoul's Place.

Ew.

So let him talk. He'd still have to prove himself in the kitchen. She'd even managed to feel the tiniest bit sorry for Alice, who'd apparently been replaced in Raoul's affections, and now had to serve him as a guest with the entire Gladiolas staff watching and whispering, remembering the scene in linen storage.

One minute until Troy was due. Darcy unlocked her front door, stood carefully on the chair with the last poster, depicting a wide range of colorful chili peppers, and measured the inches to where the top of the poster would hang, then eyeballed the spacing and hammered in the nail.

The buzz of her doorbell nearly knocked her off the chair. Butterflies were alive and well and living in her stomach; her heart pounded madly. Would she ever feel blasé about this man?

"Come in," she said in a who-can-it-be casual voice she wouldn't have thought herself capable of.

The door opened; Troy's dark head peered around its edge. He caught her eye and broke into the grin she was already wearing.

The man made her absurdly happy.

"Redecorating?" He came in, closing the door behind him.

"More like decorating." She hung the last print, studying it as if she were tremendously concerned with its placement, when she was actually overcome with a need to fling herself into Troy's arms and kiss him until he pleaded for mercy. "Martha Stewart I'm not."

"Place looks nice. You look nicer. I brought you something."

She turned and gasped with pleasure. He was holding an armful of flowers. Gladiolas, in varying shades of orange, yellow, red and white. "Oh, Troy, how gorgeous. How perfect."

"Tell me where the vases are?"

"I'll get one." She got down and dragged her stool back over to the refrigerator, touched and a little shaky.

"I never asked why you named your restaurant Gladiolas."

Darcy brought down a large wide-mouthed vase that would be perfect for the huge bouquet. "My grandfather used to grow them. He did the flowers for Mom and Dad's wedding, including a bridal bouquet of white glads. Every year my father gave my mother the flower for their anniversary."

"Romantic."

"Well…" Darcy grimaced, filling up the vase with water. "I'm sure it started out that way. By the time we were aware of the custom it was probably just grudging duty."

Troy handed her the blooms. "So I assume you know what the flower symbolizes."

"Strength, integrity and generosity."

"There's one more."

"Yes?" She waited expectantly.

"I told you Mom was a decorator. She also knew her flowers. Glads were one of her favorites." He came up behind her; his hands settled on her waist and she decided she didn't care what the last mystery characteristic of glads was because she'd just caught fire with longing.

He turned her and kissed her as if he couldn't stand being physically apart from her any more than she could.

She liked that about him.

"How did the rehearsal dinner go tonight?"

"Mmm, fine." She pressed herself against him, inhaling his clean, male scent, feeling as if she'd been starving for it. "Raoul showed up."

His body stiffened. "Why?"

"Apparently he was invited."

"How did that go?"

"I was very good. You would have been impressed. He left with all his equipment intact."

"I am impressed." His hands covered her back, stroking firmly, making her feel securely adored. "The less you react, the less power he has. How did he act?"

"He's a dick. But tonight he was a well-behaved one."

"Hmm." Troy looked thoughtful. "How do you define a well-behaved dick?"

"Not poking around where it isn't wanted." She had her hands up under his shirt, caressing the hard, satisfying planes of his chest, sprinkled with coarse hair that absolutely made male torsos as far as she was concerned.

"I'd like to show you how well-behaved mine is."

She giggled into his chest, kissing, inhaling shamelessly, using her fingers to tease his nipples. "I'd love to see that."

"Okay." Her shirt lifted over her head. His hands cupped her breasts in the thin, clingy bra she'd worn to drive him wild. "Darcy. Oh, man…"

His voice broke with passion. Apparently, the bra was doing its job.

Three seconds later, he'd wrenched up the material, baring her breasts, latched on hard and worked her nipple with his mouth. Darcy gasped, desire shooting through her. She arched back, shoving at her loose-knit pants until they fell to the floor and she could kick them off. Freed, she plunged her fingers in among his dark curls, holding him at her breast.

He made a fierce, primal noise, wrapped her in his arms and lifted. She wound her legs around him and let him carry her to the couch, thrilling at his strength. He placed her reverently on the cushion, then continued down until his breath came warm between her legs. Mouth pressed to the thin material of her panties, he blew hot, moist air that brought her to the point of desperation.

"Troy." She let her head fall back, bracing herself on her fists. "More."

"You like that?" His mouth found her again; the heat branded her.

"Yes," she gasped, squirming shamelessly on the soft fabric. "Oh, yes."

"Good." He moved her panties aside, drew his tongue across her leisurely, once up, once down, then landed on her clit and suckled until Darcy was so close to coming she could barely stay coherent.

She lifted her head, wanting him with her, and saw his

hands at his hips, jeans coming down, cock emerging proud and erect. Oh, she wanted him inside her in the worst way. No, the best. What was this man doing to her? She was crazy with lust for him, not cautious, not feeling she had to hold back her deep passion for fear of scaring him or herself.

In comparison to what had come before, everything about this relationship felt grown-up and wholesome and right.

He rolled on a condom, which was a good thing because she was so worked up she would have been tempted to tell him not to bother. She wanted him inside her without the damn condom, skin on skin, friction true and beautiful. Of course that was insanity.

He pushed inside her, face relaxing into rapture as he started to move. The condom bothered her, felt cold and artificial. She wanted warm, hot Troy inside her, wanted that joining.

What was happening? She'd sworn after the debacle with Chris never to trust a man again, never to put herself in any position where she'd be vulnerable to them. And here she was seriously considering letting this man inside her the way nature intended.

They say Chef Darcy has fallen in love.

No. Not yet, not…*no.*

"Where have you gone?" he whispered.

"Sorry." She smiled guiltily up into his face, wrapping her arms around his neck, matching his thrusts more urgently. He was so tuned into her, into her passion as well as his. That lack of self-centeredness was new, too, invasive and beautiful at the same time. "I'm back now."

"Were you back at the restaurant with Raoul?"

"Oof, no." She kissed him to stop the talking. "Don't even think that. Just…love me."

Love me? Oh, God. She'd been going to say an entirely different word, but at the last second she was afraid it would sound too coarse and had tried to substitute. Only…it didn't work.

"Relax." He was whispering, moving in delicious rhythm. "It's okay. I am loving you. Making love to you."

Yes. She closed her eyes, let her body relax, let her hands explore his muscled shoulders, the tapering lines of his back, gave herself over to his acceptance and his enjoyment of her. *Yes*.

Her body responded, climbing toward a climax that came on effortlessly and inevitably, making her tense her hips and lift toward his thrusts, greedy for the sensation, aware in her heart that he was right there with her, feeling what she was feeling, sharing every moment.

As soon as she burst over the edge, she became greedy only for his pleasure, and when he came, a new level of warmth and satisfaction spread through her, as if she'd climaxed again. Everything with Troy was so new and so different.

Last time she felt this profound a shift in her perceptions was when she got her drinking under control and applied herself to the new dream of becoming a chef, of having her own restaurant, of kicking off the influence of her bitter mother and furious father, eventually kicking off the influence of damaging men in her life, as well. Was it possible she was coming alive on a new level now? That instead of regressing into a relationship, she could view this as blossoming into one?

Being here in Troy's arms, both of them sated and blissful, she could almost believe it. Almost.

The growl of his stomach brought giggles into their afterglow and eventually got them up, dressed again and into the kitchen, where Darcy put the meal in motion.

Everything went perfectly; the hamburgers were juicy and rich, meaty with the deep flavor of the grass-fed beef boosted with porcini powder. The cheater-fries were crisp and fragrant, the coleslaw tangy and fresh-tasting. She didn't know when she'd gotten such pride from cooking such simple food. Maybe this would make another good summer special for the restaurant: Who Needs Fancy When There's Delicious?

Troy finished the last fry, swiping it in a spill of ketchup, and gave a long, satisfied sigh. "Darcy, you are a kitchen genius. I'm touched you did all this for me, especially after a long day at work."

"It was nothing." She sipped beer, realizing how much her own enjoyment of the meal had come from pleasing him. Oh, Lord, she wasn't about to get servile, was she? She wanted this new relationship to come with a guarantee the old patterns no longer applied.

He leaned back in his chair, took a sip of beer, watching her appraisingly. "You are a genius and a romantic."

"Romantic?" She gave him a good frown. "What makes you think that? Because I cooked something you like? That's my job."

"That, and you named your restaurant after the flower in your mother's wedding bouquet. If you expected love always to turn to crap, you wouldn't want to name your restaurant anything to do with disappointment and failure."

"Hmm." She considered him, slowly swinging her beer back and forth. "Interesting idea."

"Admit it. I've outed you. You're a romantic."

"Yeah?" Annoyance jabbed. She wasn't wild about being told who or what she was, even though he was right.

Wait, hadn't she been thinking how much she treasured how easily he could read her? Why was she suddenly looking for reasons to be dissatisfied?

Troy took her hand across the table, his beautiful, deep eyes so warm she had to look away. "Remember I said strength and integrity were most of what gladiolas stood for?" He squeezed her fingers. "But that there was something else, too?"

"Yes." She started feeling unaccountably nervous. "What is it?"

"Love at first sight." He spoke casually, but her hand jerked and she nearly dropped her beer, remembering that powerful first encounter at Esmee. Was that why he'd brought the flowers? Was he saying he was in love with her? Fear shot through her in the same intensity as hope.

No, no, she didn't want to be swallowed up.

Yes, yes, she was in love with him, too.

Help.

"Really." She was out of any other reaction. "Is that why you bought me glads?"

"No." He looked amused. She wasn't. "Would that scare you?"

Yes! "Why should it?"

"Because of what happened to us at Esmee." He held up his hands, smiling reassuringly. "Calm down. I know it's too soon to use words that strong."

Calm down? Wasn't she calm? She might not feel calm, but she hadn't thrown any tantrums she was aware of. "Yes, it's much too soon."

"But who knows?" His dark eyes crinkled into that sexy smile. "Maybe someday we'll look back…"

"Could be." She fidgeted under his gaze, a mass of conflict and confusion. This was not what she wanted to be talking about. "Ready for your milkshake?"

"I'm sorry." He leaned across the table to kiss her. "I didn't mean to get all intense. And yes, I am always ready for a milkshake."

"Good." She shot up from the table and crossed to the freezer, feeling jumpy and prickly. Her cell rang; she glanced apologetically at Troy. "It might be the restaurant."

He nodded, but she felt—or thought she felt—his displeasure at the interruption. She dug her phone out of her skirt pocket and checked the display. Brit, who rarely called. "It's my sister."

"It's fine. Go ahead and take it."

"Right." She hadn't asked for permission. "Hey, what's going on, Brit?"

"Have you talked to Mom or Dad lately?"

"No…" She glanced uneasily at Troy. "Why?"

"Remember that painting Dad got after the divorce that Mom kept insisting should go to her?"

"Yes…" Darcy put a hand to her abdomen, anticipating that she was going to feel sick in about three seconds. One… two…yup.

"Dad got behind again on alimony and Mom went over to his place while he was at work and helped herself. He's pressing charges."

"Oh, no." Darcy groaned and dropped her head into her hand. "When are they going to grow up?"

"You're asking me? Rudy's three and he has more sense than them."

"What are we supposed to do?"

"I'm calling Dad and persuading him to drop the charges. You call Mom and tell her to give the damn painting back. Unless you'd rather do the opposite."

"No." She got up and started pacing. This was horrible. The absolute pits. And how humiliating that Troy got to witness their family's dirty laundry in a nice big slovenly pile. "Dad deals better with you."

"Sad but true." Brit gave a long sigh. "So…how is everything going?"

Darcy laughed. "Until now?"

"Crap, I have to go, Rudy just got up. Call Mom tomorrow, then call me, would you?"

"Yeah. Okay." She ended the call, smacked the phone down on the counter.

"What's up?" He sounded wary. She didn't blame him.

"My charming parents." She yanked open the freezer, pulled out the superpremium natural vanilla and thumped it on the counter next to the blender she'd set up earlier. "Mom stole something valuable from Dad because he owes her money. He's pressing charges. Brit wants me to call Mom and convince her to return the painting."

"Why is that your job?"

She scooped up a ball of ice cream and flung it into the blender. "*Someone* has to rescue them from themselves."

"No. They own the problem."

Darcy turned to look at him, scoop raised in her right hand. "Excuse me?"

"Their problem." He set his jaw grimly, eyes hard. "Not your sister's and not yours."

"Okay. But…" She felt herself getting slightly hysterical and fought to keep it under control. What the hell did he know about her family dynamic? "Don't you think if we can keep them from making a stupid mistake, we should?"

"No, I don't. Not at all." He stared straight at her, as if he were trying to change her mind with the power of his gaze. "It might sound harsh, but I'm right in this one, Darcy."

Of course he was. Men always were. "Thanks for your opinion."

He got up slowly, towering over her, and put a hand on her arm, which she immediately wanted to shake off. "If you make that call, if you involve yourself in their crap, you'll never get out. You need to draw the line—their mess, their cleanup."

Nice. Very supportive. Is that how he'd be if she had a mess she needed help with? Your mess, your cleanup?

Please, God, don't let this relationship turn out to be typical.

Her cell rang again. Brit? She grabbed the phone, glanced at caller ID. Gladiolas. This time she didn't glance apologetically at Troy before she connected the call.

"This is Darcy."

"Chef." Ace sounded freaked out, even for him.

"Ace?" She went into instant alarm. "What happened? Why are you calling?"

"I think you'd better get over here." His voice was low, clear and deadly serious. "Now."

11

TROY DROVE HIS TOYOTA CAMRY grimly east on 94, Darcy in his passenger seat, windshield wipers attempting to compete with the downpour, his stomach pouring out acid. Darcy had insisted on going immediately to the restaurant. He wasn't sure what purpose he would serve. Supposedly he'd come to back her up, but he was having trouble giving his unconditional support to this fool's errand.

From what Troy had been able to piece together out of Darcy's near-hysterical babble, this Raoul character, who, granted, sounded like a complete waste of oxygen, had—newsflash—been in Darcy's office. Apparently, his cell had run out of batteries so he'd ducked in to use her phone, away from the kitchen noise, and this was somehow, in the logic of someone named "Ace," akin to a terrorist act.

Now they were risking a speeding ticket at close to midnight on a Saturday night when they should be in Darcy's bed, wrapped in each other's arms.

Because Ace had a bad feeling.

Troy relaxed his grip on the steering wheel, telling himself to calm down. Darcy knew Ace better than Troy did. Maybe he did have bad feelings. Maybe those bad feelings were legitimate sometimes. Or all the time. Or maybe those bad feelings came because he worked a high-stress job, ate crap and smoked his brain cells into oblivion every day. Regardless, Darcy had reacted as if she'd been told a nuclear device was found at Gladiolas and only she could defuse it.

He exited the highway, headed south on Twenty-Seventh Street to National, rain thundering on the car roof. Off they'd gone to see what Ace's bad feeling was. Troy was coming, too, because Troy was the good guy every drama queen the world over could count on to support her while she discounted whatever he had to say.

He navigated the mess that was National Avenue and followed Darcy's terse directions into the alley behind Gladiolas. Before he'd put the Camry into Park, Darcy had jumped out into the cold rain more suited to March than June. Troy turned off the engine and locked the car, resisting a childish impulse to move as slowly as possible.

Darcy wasn't Debby. He'd made it his mantra, chanted it ceaselessly, but deep down, he wasn't so sure. Maybe something important and threatening had happened. But when he'd suggested Darcy get more details from Ace before rushing off, she'd looked at him as if he'd suggested grilling a puppy.

Inside, except for the drumming of rain, the restaurant kitchen was quiet and clean, food smells light and lingering. Too bad his first glimpse of the empire Darcy ruled should be when he was indulging a terrible mood. He'd much rather be here as her special guest, celebrating her achievements with her, able to admire and compliment.

"Ace." Darcy strode toward a kid who couldn't be more than nineteen, with a mop of unruly red hair and freckles. He looked like the kid who played Ron in the Harry Potter movies. "Tell me *exactly* what happened."

"Who's he?" Ace turned his reddened narrowed eyes on Troy, whose stomach clenched, thinking of Tom. Hadn't Ace said he'd quit?

"Oh, sorry." Darcy turned back absently, gestured to Troy. "This is Troy. Troy, this is Ace, my dishwasher, sometimes line cook and right-hand man."

Apparently, Ace had a title, and Troy didn't. He gritted his teeth, trying to force himself to think more reasonably about all this. Darcy was upset. He should try to take her fears seriously even if he didn't share them.

Chilly rain dripped from his hair onto his cheek, like tears. He wiped the moisture away irritably. It was more tempting to tell Darcy to chill out, drag her home to a warm, dry bed and quiet her fears with logic and a certain technique as old as mankind.

"Ace." Darcy spoke sharply—Ace had been standing silent, in apparent weed-induced paralysis. *"What happened?"*

He came to life with a jerk. "Oh, right. So we're doing okay, the night is crazy. I'm working the line with Sean and Ben, we're keeping up, but barely. Raoul comes in again, wants to chat, hey, how are we doing, how've we been, catch him up. Like he wouldn't know it's a bad time to talk?"

Darcy shook her head, grimacing. "Of course he would."

"Now, standing here with you, chef, I'm thinking he wanted to come back while we were distracted, but at the time it didn't register."

"Of course not. You were all busy." She spoke to him as if he were a favorite pupil, making Troy mumble words no school kid should hear.

"So he says he has to make a call but his phone is dead. Sean just wants to get rid of the guy, orders are coming in like crazy, the waitresses are pissy that some plates are delayed." He looked anxiously at Darcy. "Not that it was so bad. No complaints from the customers. In fact, big tips. I think everyone had a really great time. The bride and groom came back after and—"

"*Ace,* tell the story."

"Right, sorry." Ace held up his hands. "Sean gestures Raoul back into your office to use your phone. When he comes out I realize we don't know how long he was in there. We're all in the zone."

The reefer zone?

Darcy gave Ace a don't-bullshit-me look, arms folded. "Were you smoking?"

"Not while I was on the line," Ace said proudly.

Darcy nodded approvingly. Apparently, a few hours off was a major accomplishment. "Then what?"

"Then nothing." Ace scratched the side of his head. "He leaves. We finish the shift. When things calm down and I'm closing up, I remember he was in your office and I go in. Right away I'm getting the vibe that something isn't right. Something bad is going on."

Darcy appeared to be holding her breath. Troy wiped another drip off his face. He could not believe Darcy was so enthralled with this stoner kid's big moment in the sun. Everything they'd heard so far could have waited until morning. Or afternoon. Or next week.

"What do you think happened?" Darcy asked anxiously.

"I don't know. But I'm telling you, he did something in there."

Troy wanted to laugh. "Like maybe make his phone call and come back out?"

"No." Ace shook his shaggy head. "Something else. I didn't notice anything out of place, but there was bad intent in there."

"Bad intent? That's all you've got?" Troy wanted to cry this time. "No evidence? Not even a strong suspicion?"

"You don't know Raoul." Darcy glared at Troy, who couldn't believe she was eating this up like a new dessert menu. *Bad intent?*

"Do you think he got into my computer, Ace? Could he have gotten the password?"

"I don't know." Ace's face was funereal. "I didn't touch anything. I called you right away."

Darcy rushed to the door of her office, Ace on her heels. Troy followed and parked himself outside the tiny space, leaning against the metal counter. He had a full view of the interior from here; inside, he'd only be in the way.

A minute or two ticked by while Darcy and Ace left no speck of dust unturned. Troy crossed his arms and legs, feeling more and more annoyed. His mantra was threatening to change, from *Darcy wasn't Debby* to *Yes, she was.* From everything Troy could see, history was repeating itself.

"The place looks fine. The backup flash drive is still where I hid it. Nothing seems disturbed. I can't tell if he got into the computer, though. I should think it would take time."

"This is what's driving me crazy," Ace said. "He could have been in here ten minutes or twenty or forty. You know what its like on the line. It's crazy at times."

"Does anyone know the password but you?" Troy asked.

Darcy bit her lip. "I had the file protected on the computer, but not the flash drive."

Troy bit back as much exasperation as he could. "Which wasn't disturbed. Is the password something this guy could guess?"

"No." She was emphatic. "And I change it regularly."

"Does anyone else know it?"

"Sean. He needs to know it in case I'm not around."

"Would he have anything to gain by passing it along?"

"No. And I trust him."

"So…" He was trying desperately to lead her to the obvious conclusion: *Nothing happened.* Instead, she whirled away from him and faced Ace.

"How can we find out how long he was in there? Can we

ask one of the waitresses?" Her voice was getting higher, more anxious. "Maybe Josie or Alice noticed how long he was gone from the party. We should call them now."

Troy stared at her, feeling as if he was in déjà vu hell. "It's after midnight."

Darcy gave him a look that plainly said he wasn't getting that the lives of every man, woman and child in the state of Wisconsin—no, the entire country, were at stake. "This is important, Troy."

Oh, if he had a dime for every time he'd heard that one…

"I think anyone you called would be more cooperative if you waited until morning. I know I would be."

Darcy narrowed her eyes, jammed her hands on her hips. "I'm sorry, is my livelihood being threatened an annoyance to you?"

Troy glanced at Ace. He didn't want to get into it with witnesses, but her sarcasm set him off. "Not at all. With this complete lack of evidence I don't blame you for panicking."

She took three steps, bringing her out of her office to face him toe to toe. "I told you, Raoul is a creep. I don't trust him with anything. It was a huge mistake being at all pleasant to him, and now I might have to pay for that."

"Okay." Troy pushed away from the counter, folded his arms. "Say he did take them. Then what?"

"He has my recipes and can serves my dishes, or variations of them, at his restaurant."

"And?"

She laughed incredulously. "He doesn't deserve them. They're mine."

"Agreed. What's the alternative? No one saw him. Nothing was disturbed. Will you call and ask if he took them? I'm pretty sure he'll say no. Then what? Search his restaurant? Illegal. Tattle to the newspaper? He'll spin it that you're jealous and making up lies to discredit him."

Darcy looked as if she were about to cry. "He can't get away with this."

"Get away with *what?*" He lifted his hands, let them slap down on his thighs. "We know nothing. We've proved nothing. We can't even come up with a legitimate reason to suspect anything. There is nothing we can do, especially tonight. Let's go home and go to bed for God's sake."

"That's all you can think of? Sex? My career could be going down the toilet."

Oh, for crying out loud.

"Okay." Troy backed off, hands up. "This is too weird for me. It's late, Darcy, and we're all tired and some of us are a little hysterical."

She closed her eyes, took a deep breath. "I can't leave this. I took your advice, I lowered my guard where Raoul is concerned and look what happened."

Troy stared at her. Who was this bitter woman and what had she done with playful, loving Darcy? "You're saying this was my fault?"

"Not directly."

"Even indirectly?"

"You changed me. You made me softer. People said I was becoming more human." She had her hands to her temples, looking ready to tear her hair out. "No, I mean—"

"Oh, wow, *human*. Sorry, really, that must have been horrible for you." Troy glanced at Ace, who was standing on the other side of the kitchen, head down, pretending not to listen. He moved closer to Darcy and lowered his voice. "Look, all you know is that Raoul said hi to the staff and made a phone call in your office."

She closed her eyes, took a deep breath. "Something more than that happened, Troy."

"Says a man who is out of his mind."

"He was clean when Raoul was here."

"You trust him."

She lifted her face, which even angry and frustrated, was still beautiful and still affected him deeply. "Yes."

"I'd like to be added to that list, Darcy."

"You have to earn a spot."

Troy's turn for the closed eyes and deep breath. "By unconditionally agreeing with everything you say and do?"

"By trusting *me*. Trusting that I know what I'm talking about."

He counted to three. Then five. Then ten. God help him, right now this pain was altogether too familiar. Instinct was telling him to run, far and fast, and it was shouting louder than his heart, which still wanted him to stay and protect her. How naive to expect he could heal and totally change the type of woman he went for.

"I think I should go." He had more to say, but he wasn't going to say it now, late at night in a kitchen inhabited by a psychic—or psycho—pothead.

She looked startled, then drew herself up tall. "Okay. So. I'll get a ride from Ace."

He held her gaze a few more seconds, unable to see anything but cold resolve in her eyes. Not a flicker of uncertainty or of longing. Apparently, she was not kidding when she said she regretted becoming human.

"G'night, Darcy." He walked out the back door, got nearly soaked in the few steps to his car, and pulled away from the restaurant alley in one of the foulest moods he'd been in since…

Since he was dating Debby. What a surprise. Why did the lows always come with the highs? Why couldn't he be one of those guys whose greatest moment of emotional upheaval came when his beer ran out before the football quarter did?

He drove home, scowling through the blinding thunder

of drops on the windshield. Maybe he wasn't cut out for relationships.

Or maybe Chad had been right, and he wasn't cut out for Darcy.

"EVERYTHING SEEMS TO BE shaping up perfectly." Candy lifted her face from her folder and gave a thumbs-up, nodding around their table at the Women in Power meeting to Kim, Marie and Darcy, who was trying her hardest to appear enthusiastic and interested while pain gnawed great holes inside her, like a swarm of carpenter ants hollowing out a log.

A party for married and engaged couples. What fun now that she'd believed again in the fake promise of real and permanent happiness and had it ripped away.

Whee.

"We have enthusiastic sponsors. Milwaukeedates.com of course." Candy grinned at Marie. "But also Bridal Boutique, Home Depot, Franny's Flowers and Cakewalk Cakes. They'll all donate certificates for prizes as well as help with costs. We have twenty-three confirmed couples attending and five undecided."

Darcy snorted. "Can't decide if they're coming or can't decide if they're couples?"

"Can't decide if they're coming. And of course..." Candy smiled at Darcy. "There are other couples who might become qualified in the next few weeks."

"Hmm, yes, do we know anyone like that?" Kim nudged Darcy.

"Don't think so." She pressed her lips together, brows raised, trying to appear brisk and unconcerned. That they knew she'd become involved with Troy didn't surprise her. That they assumed because she'd been with him a couple of weeks, she and Troy were on their way to the altar, did. And that she was feeling empty and sad knowing there was no way she and Troy would be at that party as any kind of couple horrified her. She didn't want to be married to Troy or anyone else. Especially not to Troy after the way he'd laughed at her fears and done nothing to help or support her when she needed him. When she left her last boyfriend, Chris, aka Mr. Cheaterpants, she'd promised herself no more men who prized only their own feelings. No matter how much she missed what was good between her and Troy, she was not going back into a relationship like that.

Frankly, she was proud of her resolve and having made the decision so quickly and forcefully to get out of yet another no-win situation, but this time before she got in any deeper.

However, the way her three friends' attention immediately zeroed in on her, she could tell she'd failed to fool them that she was fine.

"Is something wrong?" Marie, always the first to tune into people's moods.

Darcy shook her head too quickly, tears threatening; she grabbed her mug of coffee. As if that would help. "Nada."

A brief silence while they all didn't believe her. The problem with good friends was that they were good friends, and didn't put up with bull poop.

"Things tough with Troy?" Kim, uncharacteristically taking the lead. Since she'd been engaged to Nathan she'd blossomed into newfound confidence and strength—though getting the big job with Carter didn't hurt. Candy had bloomed, too, after discovering Justin.

Finding men who brought out the good in women instead of the shrewish worst was a talent that had apparently passed Darcy by.

"Things with Troy…" She bunched her mouth and shrugged as if she couldn't begin to explain or care, while traitor tears snuck into her eyes despite strict instructions to stay away.

"Uh-oh." Marie reached across the table to squeeze Darcy's

arm. Her sympathy served as an invitation for more of Darcy's tears to join the fun. "Tell us."

"Maybe we can help." Candy's brow was wrinkled in concern.

"We'd really like to," said Kim.

"Will you stop being so nice to me?" The bravest tear dared to spill over Darcy's lower lid and travel down her cheek.

So much love at the table, so much support, so many worried friends so eager to help, advise and offer comfort. Why couldn't guys behave like this when you needed them to? They were fine fixing toilets, but when it came to backing women up on emotional matters…

"Troy." She gestured helplessly. "He turned out to be a man after all."

Candy's left eyebrow rose up. "And you were hoping for…?"

"What happened, Darcy?" Kim reached for a muffin from the plate in the center of the table. "If you tell us, we can do better with our brilliant advice."

Darcy took a deep breath, fighting her instinct, which was to close up and keep her emotions private and safe, and explained as best she could. They already knew about her hopes for the restaurant, her hurt over Raoul's betrayal; she could feel them with her, murmuring support, nodding in agreement.

But as the story progressed to the events of last Saturday, she felt the sympathy and support ebbing. An exchanged glance between Candy and Marie. Kim no longer meeting her eyes.

Worse, to her ears now, Ace's suspicions sounded as paranoid and unfounded as they undoubtedly had to Troy.

Had she made a horrible mistake? Was she actually the same psycho girlfriend all her previous men accused her of being? Did she have no right to ask for Troy's unconditional support on an issue that had seemed so important and so dire at the time?

She wound up the story in uncomfortable silence, feeling shaky and disoriented, aware she was completely alone at the table of women. What was right here? What was important? Had she sacrificed her happiness with Troy for no reason? Did she have a hand in ruining all her previous relationships, as well?

"I think—" Marie spread jam carefully onto the end of a blueberry scone "—that you need to talk to Troy about this. Tell him the facts are beside the point, that you needed support and he didn't deliver."

Talk to him. Tell him what she needed. She'd done that and gotten nowhere, lowered her guard again and been punished for it. "I think I made it clear that he didn't respect my feelings."

"Did you respect his?" Marie's gentle voice carried all the power of a bazooka.

Brutal honesty time. Maybe not. She'd been so closeted in her own feelings, in her own worries, so sure she was right to panic, that no, she hadn't listened. Oh, God. She was a basket case. At very least a complete failure at relationships.

"What was he asking you to do?"

Darcy tried to block out the pain and dismay, probing her memories. He hadn't bought into her suspicions, no, but mostly he'd been trying to get her to wait until morning before pursuing the matter. To calm down and think logically about the situation and Ace's fears.

"He was asking me to pay attention, to try and look at both sides." Tears welled up, and this time she let them go. "Not so horrible, huh?"

Kim looked down with a sympathetic half smile. Candy shook her head, barely perceptible. Only Marie made full eye contact, nodding encouragingly.

"But…you know his last girlfriend was a piece of work," Candy said. "According to Justin, she was always in some crisis or other that she wanted him to fix for her."

"But this was a real threat to my business." She stopped, aware of the uneasy silence at the table. "It *felt* like a real threat to my business."

"Of course it did," Marie said. "There are no bad guys here. Only two people struggling with strong emotion."

Darcy nodded, wiping tears, fighting to get herself back under control. What now? Call Troy, apologize for overreacting, for not listening to his side? Open herself up to trying again with this wound still festering, with the underlying fear that he was liable to turn against her when she needed him? Would he even want to be with her anymore now that she'd poured such familiar poison into their well of happiness?

Her phone rang. She dug it out, feeling relief at the chance to escape the conversation. Her relief didn't last long. Ace's cell phone. Why wasn't he calling from the restaurant?

"Chef, sorry to bother, but I need to talk to you right away."

Oh, no. Darcy sighed, reminding herself to treat him with respect, but to be firm and objective, and not to let her fear carry her away this time. "What is it?"

"It's not good. Raoul's new dishwasher is Sam, who happens to be a good friend of mine. I asked a while back if he could get me an advance copy of Raoul's menu. This morning he dropped it by on his way to work."

"Okay." Her heart was pounding. She didn't even want to think about what he was going to say.

"All the specials are yours. I was right. The bastard stole them."

Darcy gasped. "Oh, my God. Ace."

Kim, Marie and Candy stopped eating and stared in alarm. Darcy looked away, unable to bear their curiosity.

"There's more," Ace said.

"Tell me."

"Sean, the only person who knew the Chef Bible file password besides you, just accepted a job as sous chef at Raoul's Place."

12

MARIE AND QUINN WALKED OUT OF the theater where they'd just seen the glorious revival of one of Marie's all-time favorite musicals, *The Sound of Music*. She'd be humming the tunes all week. "I love happy endings."

"I noticed that about you." Quinn squeezed her hand, which he'd gotten into the habit of taking when they were walking in crowds. As far as Marie was concerned, they should spend lots and lots of time walking in crowds.

They'd had a cozy drive from Milwaukee, a cozy dinner at Aria, an Asian fusion restaurant where Marie had roasted duck breast with coconut polenta that she could cheerfully drive down to eat at least once a week. Then the show. Now, maybe it was her imagination but as the evening wore on, Quinn seemed to get less and less talkative, seemed to be brooding over something. Of course Marie, with her infinitely large self-esteem, immediately had to talk herself out of the conviction that she was boring him and he was disappointed in the evening.

The good news was that once she confessed her feelings tonight—*yes, Marie and when exactly were you planning to do this?*—at least she'd be over the suspense and the worry.

Either he was open to returning those feelings someday or he wasn't.

They reached the garage in silence, got into Quinn's car in more silence. Marie arranged her skirts, buckled her seat belt, then abruptly couldn't stand it anymore. One of them had to talk.

"Party plans are going really well for the Milwaukee-dates celebration. Candy got a travel agent to donate a Caribbean cruise for an anniversary or honeymoon. Isn't that amazing?"

"That's great." His enthusiasm was honest but halfhearted. Something was definitely bothering him.

"Darcy is planning fabulous food, too. Stuffed shrimp and spring rolls, puff pastry wheels and tiny baked brie sandwiches with roasted garlic."

"Yum." He checked his rearview mirror, backed out of the space. "What's going on with her and Troy? Have they worked things out after the latest disaster?"

Marie groaned. Darcy and Troy's troubles were weighing on her. "I don't know. You saw her Wednesday when we ate at Gladiolas. She was obviously pretty miserable. She'd just found out that morning about Raoul and Sean. I don't think she's talked to Troy or that he knows yet."

"What, you haven't called to tell him?" He slowed to let another car back out of a parking space in front of him.

"I'm done meddling. I might have really messed up on this one, Quinn. I feel terrible. I should have listened to you and left it alone."

He made it the rest of the way out of the garage, paid the parking fare and emerged onto the city street. "I think you should meddle one more time."

"Say what?"

"I'm serious." He turned right, traveled the block and came to a stop at a red light. "I think Troy should know Darcy's fears were justified. He should know she's in pain. He'll want to help, and maybe they can work things out."

"Quinn." She was totally delighted. "You're as bad as I am."

"Believe it or not, I was rooting for you to succeed the whole time."

"Were you?" She smiled over at him, noticing the somber expression he'd been wearing for a while now. "Hey, are you okay? Granted I'm yapping a lot, but you've been sort of quiet since dinner."

"It's nothing." He made another turn. "I'm a little tired."

"Okay." Her spirits sank. Tired. That wasn't it.

"I was actually not looking forward to driving home. I was thinking we could—"

"Do you want me to drive?" The second the words were out of her mouth she could have kicked herself. He might have been going to suggest they—

"I was thinking we could spend the night here in town. I know a great place for breakfast. If that sounds feasible for you."

Feasible? *Feasible?*

Marie pulled herself together. Yes, she thought that plan was quite feasible. "Sure. You shouldn't be driving if you're tired."

"Right." He sounded slightly irritated. Marie wanted to reach across the car and smack him. What? He really *was* tired? That was all this overnight would be about? Not spending more time with her?

He'd given her a chaste kiss after their dinner Wednesday night at Gladiolas. Marie would have been more disappointed if she hadn't known she'd see him again tonight. And if her declaration, which she'd now decided she'd make—for sure— at the hotel, went badly, that made last Wednesday their last perfect night together as friends, which made a chaste kiss the perfect ending. Because if Quinn didn't think he could entertain romantic feelings for her, Marie was going to cut the cord completely. She couldn't bear to think of the first several Friday nights that didn't include Quinn and Roots, but...she'd survived her husband deserting her for younger blood, she'd sure as hell survive this.

If the declaration went well and Quinn responded—butterflies shimmied up her stomach and into her chest—ha! She'd be calling to thank her louse husband for leaving.

If, if, if. This was nerve-racking. So much that even she couldn't think of anything more to say. They sat in tense silence from the theater to the front entrance of the downtown Hyatt Regency—oh, my goodness—on the banks of the Chicago River just before it emptied into Lake Michigan.

This was not the type of hotel Marie generally stayed at. To put it mildly. She was more a Comfort Inn kind of girl.

"This okay? I'm a member of their frequent guest program."

"Oh, sure. I don't mind slumming occasionally."

He actually chuckled, which relieved the lines of strain around his mouth and eyes. "Good for you."

She remembered to wait for him to open her door this time, but before he made it, a uniformed employee graciously helped her out and offered Quinn valet parking, which he accepted before ushering Marie into the sumptuous glass atrium and lobby.

Small-town Midwestern girl that she was, the atmosphere of luxury and wealth was dazzling, but with Quinn at her side, not overwhelming. Maybe she'd never feel she belonged in places like this, but she would love to keep trying.

They headed for the check-in desk. Ten feet away, Quinn's steps slowed. Slowed some more. Marie slowed with him, then turned to see him looking uncertain.

Uncertain? *Quinn?*

"Two rooms, Marie?" His voice was low and gentle, but he might as well have shouted it for the way the meaning reverberated through her head. Her heart started pounding.

Two rooms, Marie?

He didn't just want to spend the night, he wanted to spend it with her.

She couldn't look at him. The emotion was so powerful, the dream held for so long unfulfilled, that she was nearly frightened.

"One is fine," she whispered.

His face relaxed; he took her hand and strode toward the front desk as if he couldn't wait to get her upstairs.

Oh, my goodness.

"Good evening sir." The reservation agent greeted them warmly, took Quinn's special guest card. "One room?"

"Yes, please. Nonsmoking."

"A king or two doubles?"

Quinn didn't even hesitate. "Two beds."

Marie went rigid. She'd assumed asking for one room meant they'd share a bed. Maybe Quinn had been thinking all along of separate beds to share platonically. Rooms here had to be extremely expensive. He was probably concerned only with saving money.

Her face flamed; her stomach turned sick with disappointment. Two beds. Quinn hadn't even blinked, hadn't even paused to consider it. She wouldn't have the nerve to tell him how she felt about him now. It would take all her courage to make it through this night, breakfast tomorrow and the long drive home.

His sweet little sister Marie. She wanted to cry so badly her throat hurt.

"We're spending the night unexpectedly. Would you have necessities sent up, please? You can check my account..."

"Absolutely, sir." The man looked at Quinn a few more

seconds, then searched his record on the computer and nodded. "I see it here. Yes, understood. We'll send that right up. You can take advantage of our laundry service, and we'll have the clothes you're in now cleaned by morning."

"Thank you."

Quinn handed over a credit card. The man tucked key cards into a tiny envelope and after asking if there was anything else they needed, pointed them to the elevators.

Marie followed Quinn numbly. Yes, there was something else she needed. But it didn't look as if she was going to get it. And if not tonight, what hope did she have for the future?

They made it to the fifth floor in agonizing silence, so uncharacteristic between them. Marie dragged herself after him down the hall, hardly even curious about the room now.

However, it was beautiful, spacious and airy, subtle colors accented with bold shades of blue, gold, burgundy and olive-green. Two damn beds, a comfortable-looking recliner, a huge flat-screen TV on a long, low credenza. Next to the door to what must be a balcony, a chair and table, on which sat a lamp and a pretty bouquet of yellow flowers Marie didn't recognize.

She tossed her purse on one of the beds and kicked off her heels, trying as hard as she could to act naturally. Little sister Marie spending the night with big brother Quinn.

"Nice room."

Quinn nodded, took off his jacket and loosened his tie. Oh, lord, at some point before sleep, he'd be taking off his shirt. His pants. Sleeping in a bed right next to hers. Waking up languid and sleep-rumpled.

Her physical longing for him became ridiculous. She wished she'd thought to ask the staff to send up sleeping pills suitable for knocking out a moose. Because she wasn't going to get a single wink tonight.

"Want to hang out on the balcony until our overnight stuff shows up?"

"Sure." Anything to get out of the bedroom and put off the strain of spending their first and last night together in total non-intimacy.

The air was chilly, a stiff wind blew toward the lake on their right. But the magnificent view of the river and Chicago's glittering downtown more than made up for the discomfort. Physically, anyway.

"Gorgeous." Marie tried to concentrate on the sights, but she was so aware of him standing next to her that she felt off balance. Good thing there was a railing or she'd pitch right off the balcony.

"It is. Are you cold?"

"A little. But only because it's freezing."

He laughed, then shocked the hell out of her by moving behind her and wrapping her in his arms. "Better?"

"Much." She could barely get the word out. He was warm and solid and sexy, and he was never going to be hers.

"Think you'll stay in Milwaukee forever, Marie?"

She shrugged, taken aback by the question. "I have no plans to leave. Why, what about you?"

"I'd like to retire somewhere warmer."

"Like?"

"The darkest jungles of Africa."

She twisted to see his face, which she could, but only barely in the dim light. "Are you serious?"

"Nope." He grinned and she managed to grin back. "I'm thinking North Carolina in the mountains. Maybe Colorado in the mountains. Or Washington State—"

"In the mountains."

"How did you know?" He rested his chin on the top of her head. "Do you like mountains, Marie?"

"I love them."

"Good."

"Why, I get to come visit?"

His arms tightened around her. "Something like that."

"Sure. I'd love that." She'd hate it. After tonight, she was—

"Do you want to sleep alone tonight, Marie?"

She stopped breathing, had to run his question through her brain again. *Did she want to sleep alone?* A buzz of pleasure and excitement chased around her body. She had to make sure there was nothing she could misunderstand, that he really meant…

Oh, Quinn.

"No," she whispered. "I don't."

"Thank God." His arms turned her in a willing circle, and he kissed her, not platonically, not sweetly, not like he'd ever kissed her before. Not like *anyone* had ever kissed her before. Passion. Intensity. Fierce desire.

For her.

He backed her into the room; she nearly tripped on the threshold; they laughed like old friends, which they were, and about to become new lovers. The mattress hit the back of her thighs and she fell onto the bed. He wasn't far behind her, covered her imperfect female body, with his magnificently male one, and she was lost in a haze of lust so strong she could barely take in what was happening.

Her hands were all over him; his were all over her. Her shirt was off. His shirt was off; she caught her breath at the sight of his chest and abdomen, still youthful and muscular.

"Marie, you are so beautiful." He unhooked her bra, lowered his mouth to her breast, groaning with pleasure.

He thought she was beautiful.

His pants were off. Her skirt was off. His briefs. Her underpants.

He was hard, smooth and beautiful, hard for *her*.

She stretched out long on the bed, wanting to minimize her

stomach, thinking she should start a serious gym regimen if she was going to be competing with—

"I have wanted this for so long." He kissed down her stomach. "So long, Marie. For months I've been wanting this, wanting you. You've been leading me in this completely sadistic dance and I've been doing everything I could think of to get you into my life, into my bed."

She was dreaming. She had to be dreaming. "Sadistic? Me?"

He was silent. Silent because he was kissing her in the most intimate way possible and she was so wildly aroused she could only lie back and let out helpless moans of pleasure. His tongue was so warm and she hadn't been touched there in so long. She was out of her mind. She wasn't going to last. He had to stop or she'd—

She clutched the bedspread and let out a sharp cry as an orgasm took her by surprise, coming on so swiftly and strong that she didn't have time to take control, to save it to share with him.

"Quinn…" She struggled to lift her head, feeling as if her body had weights on every inch. "I didn't mean to do that."

He laughed, all previous tension gone. "That felt like a mistake?"

"No." She laughed with him, stretching her arms luxuriously. "No, not at—"

A sudden knocking shocked her to sitting up in half a second. Quinn's curse shocked her into more giggles.

"Stay there." He lunged off the side of the bed, grabbed his pants and had them on in an instant, though he had some trouble getting the zipper up over his divinely wonderful erection. An erection she was going to be able to get to know intimately.

Was this really happening?

"Room service." The call came muffled through the door.

Room service? They hadn't ordered any.

"Right here." Quinn strode over, out of sight of the bed.

Marie heard the door open, heard a murmured conversation. The door closed.

"We ordered room service?"

He reappeared, pushing a cart with champagne in an ice bucket and a plate with a domed top. In his other hand, a neat little case, which she assumed held their toiletries for the night.

"Champagne and some smoked salmon?"

"Quinn." She shook her head, letting him see in her eyes how pleased and happy she was. "You seriously spoil me."

"I've been wanting to for a long time, but you're very hard to spoil."

Marie frowned. "I don't think I've ever objected. And what makes you think I'm sadistic?"

He dropped his pants, crawled toward her on the bed. "Every time I've tried to hint at my feelings for you, you've balked. I summoned all my nerve and finally kissed you after Dream Dance and you acted as if—"

"Quinn." She took his face in her hands, his beautiful, unbelievable George Clooney face, and kissed his mouth. "You told me I reminded you of your sister."

"You do. She's beautiful, strong, intelligent, funny as hell and sexy."

"And so…" She looked at him in mock horror. "You're hot for her?"

"*No.*" He scrunched up his face in disgust. "Of course not."

"See?"

"Yeah, and I remind you of your brother, remember?" He toppled her back on the mattress, covered her body again with his. "This brother you've never told me anything about. What's he like, immature and annoying?"

She giggled. "He's a complete blank."

"Oh, thanks." He pretended deep hurt. "That's just great."

Marie drew her finger down his beautiful cheek, thinking of how often she'd wanted permission to touch him like this, hardly daring to believe she had it now. "I don't have a brother, Quinn."

"Then why did you—" He rolled his eyes. "Sadism. I told you."

"Self-protection, not sadism. What about this man you were going to match me up with?"

"Oh, that." He gave a smug smile. "That was me."

"You!" She gave a shout of laughter. "You're kidding. Talk about sadism."

He kissed her mouth, traveled down into the curve of her neck. "And the problem I'd invested a lot of emotion and hope in and wasn't sure it would work out?"

"Me also?"

"You also." He returned to her lips, kissed them over and over. She wrapped her arms around his broad shoulders, still not daring to believe this was happening.

"We've wasted a long time protecting ourselves from each other," he murmured.

"When neither of us was sadistic after all."

"Neither of us." He nudged her legs apart, settled between them, erection pressing firmly against her sex, lighting her fire all over again. "Marie, I tested clean after my wife cheated, and have used condoms with every woman since. I don't want to use one with you, but I will if you'd feel more comfortable."

"I tested clean after my husband cheated, too." She lowered her eyes. "There's been no one else."

"I put nothing out there but my body, Marie." He moved up and down, rubbing her still sensitive clitoris with the hard heat of his penis. "Until I met you I didn't think anyone could touch my heart again."

"Yes." Hers swelled with happiness. She knew exactly what he meant. "I felt the same way after my marriage fell apart. It takes time to get over that kind of pain."

"We won't waste any more," he whispered.

"No." She kissed him, welcomed him into her body, into her life, into her heart and remembered what she'd promised herself she'd do tonight. "Quinn…I love you."

He stiffened. Stopped moving. She held her breath until his body continued its delicious slide inside her. "From the second or third time we met at Roots I knew I was on my way to falling in love with you, too, Marie. Since then it's only gotten stronger, week after week. I've wanted to hear you say that for so long."

"I was afraid." She looked into his eyes, moving against his thrusts, feeling happier than she ever had, and more sure than she'd ever been about anything that this man was the best thing that had ever happened to her. And maybe now, after this glorious night, she could start to believe she was the best thing for him, too.

"Don't be afraid, sweetheart. Not anymore." He put his cheek down next to hers, slid his arms underneath her. "I'm not going anywhere. Not now, not later. And if what I'm feeling tonight is any indication…not ever."

13

"HOW ABOUT THAT BREWERS' GAME last night?" Troy aimed for the basket on the guys' usual court at Kerns Park, where he met his friends regularly on Sundays for basketball games. Troy missed his shot spectacularly, though he managed to snag the rebound.

"Unbelievable contest." Kent, Kim's brother, intercepted Troy's pass to Chad, who, to everyone's relief, had replaced Kent's misogynist friend Steve in their foursome. "Fourteen innings on a zero-zero tie."

"Brewers pulled out a great win." Troy wiped sweat from his forehead. It felt good to be warm outside since the temperature had remained stubbornly below average. "I thought they were done when the Reds loaded up the bases in the twelfth."

"I was at that game." Nathan casually stole the ball from Chad and made a perfect layup. "Amazing pitcher's duel."

"Incredible." Troy caught the ball, made a halfhearted feint. He was feeling restless and crabby, not sleeping well, even his workouts weren't helping. "The crowd must have gone wild when the Brewers won."

"We missed the end."

"You didn't stay?" Troy was so appalled he stopped dribbling; Kent took advantage, grabbing the ball away to make a shot.

"We left after nine innings," Nathan said. "Kim wasn't up for it. She was tired."

"Tired?" Troy rushed to cover Kent. That's what caffeine was for. Granted it was still early in the season, but a game like that, a shutout on both sides... Troy would have given Kim the car keys and said, "Go, I'll take a taxi and catch ya later."

He caught a pass from Chad, feinted left, went right, leaving Kent in his dust, and took a shot that swished satisfyingly through the basket.

Yeah, right. More likely he would have done exactly what Nathan had: tenderly escorted his woman out of the park, even though his insides were screaming, *Nooooo!*

After his fight with Darcy a week ago, and during their mutual silence since then, the fear had taken over. He still wanted her. Still loved her. For the right or wrong reasons? He wanted to talk out the situation further, but until he had something new and constructive to add to the argument, he didn't see the point. Either they'd rehash the same conflict or talk around it, neither of which would do a damn thing for either of them or for their relationship—or whatever was left of it.

And right there was the problem. He'd just been feeling strong, back on his feet, no longer pining for Debby, understanding his patterns, and now...he was back right in it, caring so deeply for someone that all his thoughts and feelings were caught up in her 24/7. No, he hadn't gone with her when she dove off the emotional deep end, so yeah, he'd kicked that habit, but that was small comfort when he was miserable without her.

Kent caught his rebound, went over Chad's head and scored

again. They played a fairly listless game for the next half hour, then Chad picked up the ball, glanced at his watch and shot a pass to Troy. "I gotta go, guys. Bev wants to get the garden planted this weekend. We're going to Stein's nursery this afternoon."

"Ooh, hot date for Chad." Troy nodded to Nathan and Kent. "You real men up for a pint at Wolski's?"

Kent looked suddenly pained, pushed back his blond hair, squinting his blue eyes, which were so like his sister Kim's. "I, uh, have a date."

"Stein's or a real hot date?" Troy chucked the basketball at Kent, who caught it and shot it back just as hard.

"I'm seeing Lucy." He cleared his throat, grabbed the hem of his shirt and wiped his forehead. "We've been out a few times. We're meeting at four."

Troy checked his watch. Two. "So you can't go out now because..."

Kent looked mortified. "I got things to do."

Troy laughed, faked whipping the ball at him again. "What, you have to wax your legs?"

Kent rolled his eyes and headed off the court. Chad followed. Troy stood with the ball, aware he was acting nearly as badly as misogynist Steve and not caring. He gave Nathan a challenging glance. "What's your excuse?"

Nathan walked over and thumped Troy on the back. "Wedding planning. We're meeting with the florist. Like that one?"

"Jeez, what is up here?" He laughed harshly. "You guys can't pass gas without permission now?"

"Dude, we have stuff to do." Nathan left the court with the others, leaving Troy alone, feeling like the dorky kid ganged up on in the playground.

Chad gave him a withering look. "This from the guy who

when Debby ordered, 'Jump,' said, 'Into what pile of crap and how deep, dear?'"

"I'm not that guy anymore." Troy dribbled the ball a couple of times, ashamed of his outburst. Something deep and angry was being triggered by this conversation, and he needed to get it under control before he damaged friendships.

"Oh, wait a sec, wait, I recognize these symptoms. I get it now." Nathan held up his hand for attention, grinning wickedly. "Two questions. What's her name and what did she do to you?"

"Whose name?" Troy knew exactly whose, but he'd gotten locked into the sulky tough-guy act and didn't know how to break out.

"The woman who's got you so scared."

Troy dribbled the ball again. He had two choices: deny the obvious truth and dig himself deeper into being a bitter jerk, or come clean.

"Darcy Clark." There. He still felt like a jerk, but a more noble one.

"Darcy." Nathan let out a silent whistle. "No wonder. You're juggling torches, chainsaws and open gas cans."

"This still the same woman?" Chad looked disgusted. "Another manipulator bitch?"

Troy stayed silent. He didn't want to go into the problem, didn't want to hear told-you-so from Chad, or you-should-date-Bev's-boring-friend.

Nathan put his hand on his hip. "I don't know Darcy well, but she doesn't strike me as the type you want long-term, if you know what I mean."

Troy laughed bitterly, which was probably as good as saying "yes." He wanted to shout, "She's not like that," but he wasn't even sure of that much.

Chad shook his dark head in despair. "Here we go again."

Kent walked back toward Troy, held out his hands for his basketball. "I have time for a beer."

Troy tossed him the ball, feeling even more like a jerk in the face of his friend's graciousness. "You don't have to if you're busy."

"I have time. Lucy will just have to deal with my hairy legs." He rolled his eyes, smacking Troy's shoulder. "Come on."

Troy followed him off the court toward Nathan and Chad and gave them a quick nod. "Sorry for the crap."

"No problem, man."

"Forget it."

Fist-bumps and back slaps cemented the apology, then Nathan and Chad went off to their cars, while Troy and Kent drove in Troy's Camry to Wolski's, where they ordered beers and settled into a booth. After a few uncomfortable comments about Milwaukee's sports teams and the unusually cool weather, they sat in awkward silence. Not drinking.

Finally, Kent pushed aside his beer. "Look, I suck at talking about this feelings stuff. I hung out with people like Steve for so long I bought into their macho bull about women. Then I met Lucy, and it was like…I dunno, a goddamn thunderbolt."

Troy didn't know whether to laugh or groan. "Let me guess. She lit you up the second you laid eyes on her? It was as if your nerve endings were coming alive for the first time ever? Like a life heat?"

Kent looked astonished. "Yeah. How did you— Oh, Darcy?"

Troy nodded grimly. "Yup."

"Man, it's like some chick flick. I hate chick flicks. But she changed my life. This feeling changed my life. I can't deny that. Everything I thought I knew about women and about me…" He shook his head in awe. "Steve didn't have a clue.

Making Lucy happy isn't about weakening me, because what makes her happy makes me happy."

Troy could not believe he was sitting here listening to Kent wax poetic about love. "Okay."

"And she feels the same way." He gulped beer, looking uncomfortable. "I sound like Dr. Phil, huh?"

"I promise I will tell no one."

"Thanks." He grinned wryly. "But you know what Steve was most wrong about? I don't feel less of a man enjoying her and the things she enjoys. I feel more. Like my dick is bigger."

"Oh, oh." Troy cringed, waving Kent away like a bad smell. "I could *really* do without that image."

"Figuratively, anyway, but it is." Kent dragged his beer closer. "Point is, if it's good, you don't feel like you *have* to do that stuff, the flowers and the gardening. You want to."

"Even leaving an extra innings game after the ninth?"

"Ooh." Kent screwed up his face in pain. "There are limits. But Debby was serious poison—don't judge anything by her. We've all dated Debbys, women who trample men. A good woman will lift you up to something higher and better."

Troy cracked up. "Thank you, Preacher Kent. How are things at the Church of Feelings?"

Kent joined in the laughter. "I'm born again, brother Troy! Halle-freaking-lujah."

"Amen to that." Troy lifted his beer. They toasted and drank.

"I take it you and this Darcy woman fought."

"She got upset about something and I didn't see the point. Reminded me of Debby and I freaked."

"Hmm." Kent stroked his chin thoughtfully. "Is she like Debby when things are good?"

Troy didn't even have to think about that one. "Not at all. Night and day."

"Remember Steve's theory that falling for a woman meant handing her your balls?"

"Yup." Troy moved uncomfortably. "Exactly the phenomenon I'm trying to avoid repeating."

Kent shook his head. "I have a new theory. This one is a hell of a lot better."

"Okay." Troy lifted an eyebrow. This would be good. "I'm ready, let's hear it."

"My theory is that when you fall for a woman, you don't hand her your balls, you offer them."

Troy made a face. "And this is different how?"

"Because if she's a real woman, a good woman, a woman worth keeping—" Kent leaned back smugly in the booth "—she isn't going to want them."

TROY KNOCKED ON THE BACK DOOR to Gladiolas. Darcy wouldn't be there, which he was counting on, but he remembered her talking about a special event they were holding that night, which the restaurant, usually closed on Mondays, would be open for. He wanted to talk to Ace. Marie had called him the night before and dropped the bomb about Sean's betrayal and the proof that Raoul stole her recipes. Troy had been trying to figure out how to help Darcy before Marie even finished the story. Though whether or not Raoul had turned out to be criminal as well as an asshole was beside the point. The point was that Darcy had strong feelings, and he'd rejected them out of selfish fear and baggage courtesy of a completely different woman. That much at least he could fix. The rest…he'd try.

"Yeah?" Ace met him with a challenging stare out of eyes that appeared clear and in touch with reality. Good for him. And good for Troy, who didn't want to deal with a clouded mind. "Darcy's not here."

"I know. I want to talk to you."

Ace's reddish brows lowered; he hesitated, obviously struggling between loyalty and curiosity. "About what?"

"Can I come in?"

Another once-over. Good that he was so protective of Darcy, but Troy needed him on his side today. "Do you need to?"

"I owe you an apology. If I have to humble myself, I'd like to do it somewhere other than a cold alley that smells like kitchen castoffs."

The corners of Ace's mouth twitched. "I don't know, dude. I'm thinking you can't get much more humble than that."

"True." He waited, staring Ace down.

"Okay." Ace stepped aside, gestured him in. "C'mon. Not too busy at the moment, but it won't stay that way."

Troy stepped into the kitchen, feeling an intense pang of missing Darcy from being on her beloved turf, and of guilt that last time he'd been here he'd failed to appreciate it or her.

"So?" Ace took up a chef's knife, started rapid-fire chopping onions. "What's up?"

"I was an ass the other night."

"No argument here." Ace gathered the minced onions onto the knife and deposited them smoothly into a bowl.

"I didn't listen, thought she was overreacting. And you."

"Yeah, I got that loud and clear. You hear what happened?"

"Yes."

"I was right. I told you. Bad intent. I picked up on it like radar."

Troy gritted his teeth, telling himself to be patient. "I want to help Darcy."

Ace smirked, took another onion, whacked it in half with more force than necessary and started slicing. "How can *you* help her?"

Troy couldn't hold back a noise of exasperation at his attitude. "You know anyone in Raoul's kitchen?"

"Yeah." The answer came out grudgingly.

"How well?"

Ace's eyes narrowed. "How well do you need me to know them?"

Troy sighed, leaning forward, hands on the edge of the gleaming counter. "Well enough to let us in for a few hours when there's no one else there. Soon. Like, tonight."

Ace considered him for a long minute. "This sounds illegal."

"Yeah, and you never break the law." He put his fingers together at his lips, mimicking someone smoking a joint.

Ace shoveled more perfectly diced onion into the bowl. "I'm trying to quit."

"Good for you."

"I already have, actually. For the most part. I want to be a chef someday. Darcy talked to me, said I can't do it stoned. She was right. She's awesome."

Troy hid a smile. Good. He had the kid talking. "She's a smart lady."

"She's also really talented, and she works incredibly hard. She's worked incredibly hard to get all this." He waved his knife around the kitchen. "Nothing was handed to her. Not like some people."

Someone besides Troy had a pretty big crush on Darcy Clark. "You mean Raoul."

Ace made a scornful noise. "He's not a chef. He's a con man. Takes orders, but can't cook for shit. Sean was like that, too. I hope they go down together."

"I think we can make sure they do."

"Yeah?" Ace's suspicion melted into eagerness. "What are you planning?"

"Nothing much. I need access to his computer for a couple of hours when no one else is around. And I could use someone with me who has cooking smarts."

Ace's smile started out small, then grew into a full-blown grin that bubbled over into a chuckle. "Dude."

"You with me?" Troy held up his hand.

Ace high-fived him enthusiastically. "I can get you exactly what you need."

14

DARCY OPENED HER FRONT DOOR, reached down to collect her paper and stopped halfway. Wow! It was warm! It was *gorgeous*. It was as if the hellish spring they'd been suffering through, all the rain and clouds and cold, had finally been vanquished overnight, the result of some spectacular final battle with summer emerging victorious. Nine o'clock in the morning and it must be seventy already. Sunny. Dry. A cool breeze bringing scents of growing and green.

Oh, what a blissful rebirth, and just in time. Because if a whole lot more kept going wrong, Darcy was going to quit this world and start her own planet.

She picked up the paper, brought it inside and went through the house, throwing open windows, inhaling huge lungfuls of the wonderful, sweet air pouring in. Mid-June for crying out loud. This was more like it.

If only the rest of her world would come around so perfectly and completely. The last week or so had been an exercise in pain and frustration. Sean was gone, she'd bumped Ben up to sous chef and Ace, bless his heart, to Ben's position as assistant cook. She could see that kid going places soon. Already, his skills were developing as well as his confidence, and all with a clear head. She'd found a new dishwasher fairly easily to replace him. Gladiolas would be okay.

What still hurt was Sean's betrayal. That he'd taken a job with Raoul wasn't so terrible. Each man for himself, and poaching employees went on in the restaurant business all the time.

But did he have to take her recipes with him?

Apparently. Raoul undoubtedly offered a nice bonus if Sean came to work with menu in hand. Saved Raoul having to provide anything like talent or originality. Which he wouldn't get from Sean, either, her only satisfaction. Once they went through her files, they'd have to change strategies.

But okay, enough brooding. It was a beautiful day, and as Troy had pointed out, there was nothing she could do about the situation but forge on with her own work as best as she could.

On her way to open the last window in her bedroom, the phone rang.

"Darcy, it's Brit."

Darcy closed her eyes. She hadn't called her mother. Brit would be annoyed. "Hi, there."

"Mom hasn't heard from you."

"No."

Her sister made a sound of exasperation. "The situation is becoming ridiculous."

"The situation has *always* been ridiculous."

"You need to talk to her. Dad won't drop the charges until she at least apologizes."

Darcy walked over to her bed and sat down. Something was really bugging her about this situation, and she needed time to examine it. "Really."

"They're in a total stand-off. Acting like children."

Darcy frowned up at the picture she had framed on her dresser. Mom and Dad, smiling, arms around each other and around Darcy and Brit. They'd used the picture as a Christmas card probably twelve or thirteen years ago. A photographer's pose, with show-our-family's-love smiles. Fake love. How long did her parents hold out before they gave up on loving each other?

"Don't you think it's time they acted like adults?"

"Yeah? Hey, good idea, Darcy." Brit's voice dripped sarcasm. "Why don't you suggest that?"

"I'm not going to suggest anything." She rose from the bed, breathing in the earthy, rich scents of summer, feeling powerful and free. Troy had been right. This issue had nothing to do with her. "They own the problem. They need to fix it. We're not helping them if we keep stepping in. Let them deal with it."

"Darcy! Mom could go to jail. You want her to go on trial?"

"She and Dad divorced years ago. Why should you and I keep being punished for this?"

"I can't believe you're not going to help."

"Why should I?"

"Because it's what people who love each other do."

Tears rose in Darcy's eyes. No. Not always. "Sometimes you have to let them help themselves. This is one of those cases. They loved each other deeply enough to get married all those years ago. Just because that love didn't last—"

"Huh?" Her sister sounded taken aback. "They never loved each other deeply."

Darcy blinked. "What are you talking about?"

"You didn't know? Mom married Dad to get away from home. You know about Grandpa's drinking. She didn't take long to figure out she'd gotten out of the fireplace into the fire. She said she stood at the altar and recited her vows feeling panicky and sick to her stomach."

Darcy sat back down on the bed, stunned. "Did Dad love her?"

"They barely knew each other, Darcy. I can't believe no one told you this." Brit's voice gentled. "I assumed you knew. Mom was pregnant, so they had to get married fast. She lost the baby a month later."

Darcy put a hand to her head. "Why did she tell you this and not me?"

"She told me when I got married. She wanted me to be absolutely sure about Jason."

"Were you?" Darcy held her breath. Her sister's answer mattered hugely.

"Absolutely. I had no doubts at all." Brit spoke with total confidence. "Everything about being with Jason felt different from any boyfriend I'd had before, and not just because I was sober. I was a better, stronger person around him. I could tell him anything, and trust me, there was a lot of bad stuff to tell. He took it all in stride. Even though we fought, and still do, I know he has me at the top of his list all the time."

Everything felt different. She could tell him everything. He took it all in stride. But was Darcy at the top of Troy's list? He'd been at the top of hers.

She closed her eyes. Maybe she could be more confused, but she didn't think so.

"I'll call Mom."

"Oh, Darcy. Thanks, honey. Thank you so much." Brit's words came out in a breathless rush. "I love you."

"Love you, too."

She punched off the call. Stared at the phone for a few seconds, then dialed. She wasn't going to deliver the message Brit wanted, but she was going to speak to her mother.

Half an hour later, she finished the call. Everything Brit said was true. Her parents' love hadn't turned to crap, it had been crap to begin with. All her adult life, until the divorce,

Darcy's mother had been miserable, because she'd listened to her head instead of her heart and went through with the marriage, doomed from the start.

Darcy roused herself and opened the window in her bedroom, leaned on the window and breathed in and out steadily, rapturously. What did her heart say?

"Oh." She jumped and bumped her head painfully on the sash. Troy's car coming up the street.

Was it his Camry? It had to be. Tall single male occupant, gray car, slowing, then parking outside her house.

She ducked, then peered up over the edge of the sill, unable to keep from looking.

Troy. Getting out of the car. Striding up her front walk carrying a grocery bag, wearing shorts and a T-shirt.

Oh, my.

She was toast. Why was it that she could have had every possible legitimate and sound reason to stay away, to resist him, to keep herself from entertaining even the possibility of resuming their relationship, but one look made her entire body convulse with longing?

Or maybe just her heart.

She ran to the front door, slowed two steps from it and waited for the bell, which took several long seconds. Was he nervous? He couldn't be any more nervous than she was.

Ding-dong. Finally. She waited several seconds herself, then opened, not bothering to look surprised.

"Hi." She met his eyes and the impact was as strong as it had been that first night at Esmee. *Aw, hell.*

"Hi." He was smiling at her, and she could do nothing but smile back. In one second it seemed everything they'd fought over was ridiculous, that nothing mattered but the depth of this feeling. The depth of quiet certainty that he was someone she desperately wanted to be close to in all ways for all time. Was this what Brit meant?

"What are you doing here?"

He held up the grocery bag. "Potato chips and Diet Coke. You said it was your favorite meal, eaten on the beach. It's beach weather, so I thought you might like to go."

His voice was confident, his stance solid, but she caught the vulnerability in his eyes that shot arrows right into her heart. She couldn't refuse him anything, even if she wanted to.

She didn't. "That sounds pretty nice."

The grin that crossed his face made her whole world sing. "I have stuff to tell you, to talk about. To apologize for."

"So do I."

His smile grew brighter, sweeter. "Then let's go."

They drove to Bradford Beach on the shore of Lake Michigan in silence unbroken after a stilted conversation about the weather and how glad they were summer seemed to be arriving at last. There was too much to say, nowhere to begin to say it. But they were together, and Darcy was feeling full and happy, and it had been a long while since she'd felt that way. Like since the last time they were together.

Her mother had never felt this. She was suddenly more sure of that than she'd ever been of anything.

They parked and trudged over the warm sand to a likely spot, where Troy spread out a blanket and joined her on it, handed her a can of cold soda and opened the bag of chips. She ate a handful, following the salty crunch with sweet, bubbly cola. The sun shone on tiny waves covering the lake, making them sparkle. Milwaukee's residents had come out, moles from underground, to worship the delayed change in season. Kids ran around shouting, Frisbees flew. A few brave souls dared to enter the water, which would still be icy from the long winter and cold spring.

"This is perfect."

"I think so." He grinned at her. "But any place with you would be."

"And potato chips."

He touched her shoulder playfully. Even that tiny touch made her melt with longing. "I guess Raoul's Place will be opening soon."

"I guess." She was surprised he'd bring up the topic that way. Almost cheerfully.

"I'm kind of looking forward to it."

She sent him a sidelong look. What the hell? "Really?"

"Really." He looked smug, tossing back chips that would have zero effect on his incredibly toned body. "I have a strong feeling the opening is going to be a disaster."

Something in his voice made her sit up and take notice. "What makes you say that?"

He shrugged. "I have this *feeling*."

"You have a feeling?" She had no idea what to make of this.

"Sure. Ace's not the world's only psychic."

"Okay…" She gestured, coaxing out his next words. "So what is this *feeling?*"

"I don't think the dishes Raoul stole from you are going to fly at all."

Darcy narrowed her eyes. "Why not?"

"I don't *really* know, but I have a strong premonition that the recipes in his computer aren't the ones he stole from you."

She put her can down on the ground, excitement thrumming through her. "They're not."

"They're close, probably. But on each one, some ingredients and amounts are different. Almost as if they'd been changed."

"Changed." Her brain was whirling. He was getting at

something, something she was starting to understand she'd really, really like. "Who would do something like that?"

"Gosh, I have no idea. Someone who could get into his place after closing. And someone with pretty strong computer skills."

"You and Ace."

He gave her a look of horror. "Me? Ace? Absolutely not. We would never do anything illegal and satisfying and incredibly enjoyable like that. At least I wouldn't. Particularly not to protect and avenge the woman I love."

"You *broke* in and—" Darcy stopped in shock. "Did you say the woman you love?"

"Oh, that, yeah." He drank a few swallows of soda. "I can't promise our scheme will totally ruin his opening. But it will certainly throw a wrench into the works. And maybe teach him a lesson. Maybe."

Darcy threw her arms around him and knocked him back onto the sand, spilling both their drinks. "I just care that you believed me. That you went out of your way, out of your comfort zone to help me. And that you love me."

His eyes were clear and bored straight into hers. "I do, Darcy. I love you."

"I love you, too." The words were easy to say because they were so entirely true. "I can't believe you did all that for me, Troy. I can't tell you what it means to me."

"Well." He stroked her hair, then down to her neck and across her back. Oh, the way this man touched her... "There is something you can do for me."

She grinned, moving her hip so it made contact with his fly. "Really? What's that?"

His smile faded into seriousness; he rolled her over onto her back. "Come to Marie's party with me, Darcy. Officially."

Her eyes widened; she couldn't move. She stared at him

unblinking. Officially. To the party for engaged and married couples.

"Um, Darcy?"

She couldn't speak. Emotions were jamming her voice box.

"You okay?"

"Ungyuh."

"Did you get that I just asked you to marry me?"

Tears rose, started rolling down her temples. One landed into her ear. She giggled, then let out a sob, unable to sort out her reactions. He'd asked her to marry him. Offering to put her at the very top of his list. Wasn't it too soon?

She checked in with her heart. It was nothing but happy and at peace with the idea.

She understood.

He kissed her forehead, her cheeks, her eyelids, then a long sweet kiss on her lips that made her moan with the pleasure of tasting him again. "Does looking as if you have serious indigestion mean yes?"

Now she couldn't stop smiling, aware she was taking an absurdly long time to answer. Same way she'd taken forever to respond a month ago when he asked her at Esmee if he could buy her a drink. When she'd fallen in love with him at very first sight. And oh, what a life-changing answer that turned out to be.

"Or…no?"

This moment was life-changing, too. She was looking toward eternity with a man who was male every way she'd dreamed a man could be. Strong enough to tell her when she was wrong. Strong enough to admit when he was. Caring enough to put himself on the line to ensure she was protected, to make sure she felt loved and adored.

There was only one answer to give.

She pulled his head down to her, kissed his sexy mouth,

following the certainty in her heart that this time she'd found love that would stay this beautiful, strong and full of joy forever.

"Yes."

Epilogue

"WHAT IS THAT ON YOUR FINGER, young lady?"

"That?" Marie blinked innocently at Darcy. "Oh, that's Quinn's fortieth birthday present to me. My engagement ring. Like it?"

"Your what?" Darcy shrieked so loudly Candy and Kim immediately detached themselves from their nearby conversations and came running over.

"What is it?"

"Check this out." Darcy grabbed Marie's hand and showed the ring around. "Mrs. Quinn Peters-to-be."

"Marie!" Candy flung her arms around her. Kim beamed and took her turn next.

Darcy kissed her on both cheeks, French style, then added a fierce hug. "It's about time. I didn't think you'd *ever* admit that you wanted a man in your life, missy."

"Okay, okay." Marie's smile stretched ear to ear; she glanced at Quinn. Was it her imagination or did he look even more movie-starlike than usual? She'd finally relaxed into the reality that he loved her, and she couldn't believe how much she was looking forward to their life together. "Guess it was time to practice what I preached, huh?"

"Obviously." Darcy sent Troy yet another I-love-you look.

Marie couldn't believe the instant change in her. In the last few days since Darcy had finally stopped fighting what she felt for Troy, a lifetime of suppressed warmth had been pouring out of her. She seemed to adore everyone and everything. In fact, she could compete with Kim and Candy in the nauseatingly-in-love department. And with Marie, who had never thought she could be this happy again.

"When are you getting married, Marie?" Kim asked.

She beamed at Quinn, who interrupted his conversation to beam right back. "As soon as possible."

"Honeymoon?" Darcy asked.

"Oh, nothing much. London, Sydney, Paris and ending up with a week on St. Thomas."

The girls squealed.

"Rough, rough times," said Candy, without a trace of envy. In fact, Darcy and Kim looked nothing but happy for her, too. Good friends, all of them. She was so glad she'd been able to help them find love—and herself in the process. A miracle she'd never take for granted.

"It is rough." Marie bowed her head meekly. "But I will have promised myself for better or worse, so I feel bound to put myself through it."

"You are a saint." Candy patted her shoulder.

"Darcy, have you and Troy set a date yet?"

Darcy shook her head, glowingly happy, the same face Marie saw each time she looked in a mirror. "Too much upheaval ahead. I'm in no hurry and neither is Troy. I'll sell my house and move in with Troy as soon as possible, then we'll wait until Gladiolas is settled in its new location. When we can breathe again, we'll pick a date and do it quietly, preferably somewhere warm."

"That sounds perfect," Kim said. "Anyone else with news? Seems it's all good these days."

"Me!" Darcy raised her hand like a schoolgirl. "Troy heard

that the preorders for his and Justin's book have been really strong."

"Yes!" Candy clapped her hands. "Stronger even than the publisher hoped, which is awesome. Except it means they're going to have to write another one, and will therefore be working hard and not able to attend to our every need as they should."

"It's shameful." Darcy shook her head.

"Speaking of shameful, I heard the tragic news about Raoul's restaurant." Marie tsk-tsked, unable to hide her pleasure. "*Such* a sad tale."

"I know." Candy put on a hushed voice suitable for a funeral—for someone she'd wanted dead all along. "Imagine, all that excitement, and just before opening, his investor is arrested for embezzlement and turns out to be bankrupt."

"It just breaks my heart," Kim added with unmitigated delight. "Though I don't think Raoul's Place was long for this world anyway. I read reviews and it seems none of the specials were any good. Seems none of the flavor combinations or seasonings worked for the reviewer. Wasn't that odd?"

"You know—" Darcy held out her hands "—some people have it. Some don't. I guess he just didn't."

The women dissolved into giggles, helped no doubt by the champagne and happiness flowing freely in the room.

"When are you moving Gladiolas, Darcy?" Candy asked.

"Next month. I did poor Raoul a big favor, out of the infinite goodness of my heart." She put on a noble martyr face. "Gladiolas is taking over the space he had to forfeit when he went under. Quinn handled it all. We got it for practically nothing. If things go well, we might open a second location next year."

"Oh, you are a saint, too, helping the poor man sell his property vastly undervalued." Candy couldn't control her giggles. "It's amazing how everything has worked out for us over the past six months. All our lives are so different now. So much happier."

Marie didn't hide her satisfaction. "Getting the three of you matched up was my New Year's resolution. Probably the first one I ever stuck to."

"No way. Well, here's to you, Marie, for being a wonderful meddling pain in the ass." Darcy toasted her with champagne. "Thank you for making such happiness possible for all of us."

"Amen," Kim said. "And how great that you found some for yourself, as well."

"Hear, hear." Candy raised her glass. "Here's to many years of bliss and lots of babies."

Kim giggled. Marie nearly spit out her champagne. "Watch what you say, honey."

"Marie, you're forty, not ninety," Darcy said.

"You think it's such a great idea, *you* have the babies."

She waited for Darcy to start shrieking her usual objections and was stunned when she shrugged mildly and blushed. "Maybe I will someday."

Okay. Pigs had to be flying around here somewhere.

"You'd be a great mom," Candy said. "Have a daughter and cook with her in the kitchen."

Darcy's eyes took on a faraway look. Marie was flabbergasted. This was more of a miracle for Darcy even than she'd thought possible. She'd have to tell Quinn. Now she could tell him everything, all day long. Could and wanted to and did. Poor man.

The party wound down, prizes were won by elated couples, Darcy's excellent hors d'oeuvres polished off, the last glass of champagne drunk.

Candy and Justin left, arms linked. Kim and Nathan left, holding hands. Darcy and Troy went back into the kitchen, arms around each other, Troy's hand making its way down to Darcy's rear, then back up, then back down.

Marie smiled and leaned into Quinn's strong arms. "Ready to go?"

"I'm ready." He kissed her. "Have I told you how beautiful you look tonight?"

"Only about five times."

"Oops." He cringed comically. "I'm slipping."

"The romance is clearly over."

"Never." He grinned and offered her his arm. "Shall we?"

"Let's." She took his arm, thrilled as usual by the strength of the muscle underneath his sleeve. When they got to his house, she had plans for this man that would last all night long, as she was sure Candy had for Justin. And Kim for Nathan. And Darcy for Troy.

All night long tonight, tomorrow and for the rest of their lives.

* * * * *

Harlequin Blaze

COMING NEXT MONTH

Available June 28, 2011

#621 BY INVITATION ONLY
Lori Wilde, Wendy Etherington, Jillian Burns

#622 TAILSPIN
Uniformly Hot!
Cara Summers

#623 WICKED PLEASURES
The Pleasure Seekers
Tori Carrington

#624 COWBOY UP
Sons of Chance
Vicki Lewis Thompson

#625 JUST LET GO...
Harts of Texas
Kathleen O'Reilly

#626 KEPT IN THE DARK
24 Hours: Blackout
Heather MacAllister

You can find more information on upcoming
Harlequin® titles, free excerpts and more at
www.HarlequinInsideRomance.com.

REQUEST YOUR FREE BOOKS!
2 FREE NOVELS PLUS 2 FREE GIFTS!

◆Harlequin® *Blaze*™

red-hot reads!

YES! Please send me 2 FREE Harlequin Blaze® novels and my 2 FREE gifts (gifts are worth about $10). After receiving them, if I don't wish to receive any more books, I can return the shipping statement marked "cancel." If I don't cancel, I will receive 6 brand-new novels every month and be billed just $4.24 per book in the U.S. or $4.71 per book in Canada. That's a saving of at least 15% off the cover price. It's quite a bargain. Shipping and handling is just 50¢ per book in the U.S. and 75¢ per book in Canada.* I understand that accepting the 2 free books and gifts places me under no obligation to buy anything. I can always return a shipment and cancel at any time. Even if I never buy another book, the two free books and gifts are mine to keep forever.

151/351 HDN FC4T

Name	(PLEASE PRINT)	
Address		Apt. #
City	State/Prov.	Zip/Postal Code

Signature (if under 18, a parent or guardian must sign)

Mail to the **Reader Service:**
IN U.S.A.: P.O. Box 1867, Buffalo, NY 14240-1867
IN CANADA: P.O. Box 609, Fort Erie, Ontario L2A 5X3

Not valid for current subscribers to Harlequin Blaze books.

Want to try two free books from another line?
Call 1-800-873-8635 or visit www.ReaderService.com.

* Terms and prices subject to change without notice. Prices do not include applicable taxes. Sales tax applicable in N.Y. Canadian residents will be charged applicable taxes. Offer not valid in Quebec. This offer is limited to one order per household. All orders subject to credit approval. Credit or debit balances in a customer's account(s) may be offset by any other outstanding balance owed by or to the customer. Please allow 4 to 6 weeks for delivery. Offer available while quantities last.

Your Privacy—The Reader Service is committed to protecting your privacy. Our Privacy Policy is available online at www.ReaderService.com or upon request from the Reader Service.

We make a portion of our mailing list available to reputable third parties that offer products we believe may interest you. If you prefer that we not exchange your name with third parties, or if you wish to clarify or modify your communication preferences, please visit us at www.ReaderService.com/consumerchoice or write to us at Reader Service Preference Service, P.O. Box 9062, Buffalo, NY 14269. Include your complete name and address.

HB11

USA TODAY *bestselling author B.J. Daniels*
takes you on a trip to Whitehorse, Montana,
and the Chisholm Cattle Company.

RUSTLED

Available July 2011 from Harlequin Intrigue.

As the dust settled, Dawson got his first good look at the rustler. A pair of big Montana sky-blue eyes glared up at him from a face framed by blond curls.

A woman rustler?

"You have to let me go," she hollered as the roar of the stampeding cattle died off in the distance.

"So you can finish stealing my cattle? I don't think so." Dawson jerked the woman to her feet.

She reached for the gun strapped to her hip hidden under her long barn jacket.

He grabbed the weapon before she could, his eyes narrowing as he assessed her. "How many others are there?" he demanded, grabbing a fistful of her jacket. "I think you'd better start talking before I tear into you."

She tried to fight him off, but he was on to her tricks and pinned her to the ground. He was suddenly aware of the soft curves beneath the jean jacket she wore under her coat.

"You have to listen to me." She ground out the words from between her gritted teeth. "You have to let me go. If you don't they will come back for me and they will kill you. There are too many of them for you to fight off alone. You won't stand a chance and I don't want your blood on my hands."

"I'm touched by your concern for me. Especially after you just tried to pull a gun on me."

"I wasn't going to shoot you."

Dawson hauled her to her feet and walked her the rest of the way to his horse. Reaching into his saddlebag, he pulled out a length of rope.

"You can't tie me up."

He pulled her hands behind her back and began to tie her wrists together.

"If you let me go, I can keep them from coming back," she said. "You have my word." She let out an unladylike curse. "I'm just trying to save your sorry neck."

"And I'm just going after my cattle."

"Don't you mean your boss's cattle?"

"Those cattle are mine."

"*You're* a Chisholm?"

"Dawson Chisholm. And you are…?"

"Everyone calls me Jinx."

He chuckled. "I can see why."

*Bronco busting, falling in love…it's all in a day's work.
Look for the rest of their story in*

RUSTLED

*Available July 2011 from Harlequin Intrigue
wherever books are sold.*

Copyright © 2011 by Barbara Heinlein

Looking for a great Western read?

We have just the thing!

A Cowboy for Every Mood

Visit
www.HarlequinInsideRomance.com

for a sneak peek and exciting exclusives
on your favorite cowboy heroes.

Pick up next month's cowboy books
by some of your favorite authors:

Vicki Lewis Thompson
Carla Cassidy
B.J. Daniels
Rachel Lee
Christine Rimmer
Donna Alward
Cheryl St.John
And many more…

Available wherever books are sold.

ACFEM0611R

Harlequin *Desire*

ALWAYS POWERFUL, PASSIONATE AND PROVOCATIVE.

USA TODAY BESTSELLING AUTHOR

MAUREEN CHILD

DELIVERS AN UNFORGETTABLE STORY IN A NEW TEXAS CATTLEMAN'S CLUB MINISERIES

ONE NIGHT, TWO HEIRS

Marine officer Rick Truitt is shocked to learn the truth…he's fathered twin girls. With his past love and now mother of his children, Sadie Price, back in town, he's bound to do the honorable thing and propose marriage. But will Sadie be able to let her guard down and accept Rick's offer?

Available July wherever books are sold.

— www.Harlequin.com —

SD73109

THE NOTORIOUS
WOLFES

A powerful dynasty, where secrets and scandal never sleep!

Eight siblings, blessed with wealth, but denied the one thing they wanted—a father's love. Haunted by their past and driven to succeed, the Wolfes scattered to the far corners of the globe. It's said that even the blackest of souls can be healed by the purest of love....

But can the dynasty rise again?

Beginning July 2011

A NIGHT OF SCANDAL—*Sarah Morgan*
THE DISGRACED PLAYBOY—*Caitlin Crews*
THE STOLEN BRIDE—*Abby Green*
THE FEARLESS MAVERICK—*Robyn Grady*
THE MAN WITH THE MONEY—*Lynn Raye Harris*
THE TROPHY WIFE—*Janette Kenny*
THE GIRL THAT LOVE FORGOT—*Jennie Lucas*
THE LONE WOLFE—*Kate Hewitt*

8 volumes to collect and treasure!